THE Littlest Rebel

Shirley Temple EDITION

THE
Littlest Rebel

by EDWARD PEPLE

With illustrations from the motion picture
featuring **SHIRLEY TEMPLE**

RANDOM HOUSE, NEW YORK

THE Littlest Rebel

Chapter One

Young Mrs. Herbert Cary picked up her work basket
and slowly crossed the grass to a shady bench under-
neath the trees. She must go on with her task of plan-
ning a dress for Virgie. But the prospect of making her
daughter something wearable out of the odds and ends
of nothing was not a happy one. In fact, she was still
poking through her basket and frowning thoughtfully
when a childish voice came to her ears.

"Yes, Virgie! Here I am. Out under the trees."

Immediately came a sound of tumultuous feet and
Miss Virginia Houston Cary burst upon the scene. She
was a tot of seven with sun touched hair and great dark
eyes whose witchery made her a piquant little fairy. In
spite of her mother's despair over her clothes Virgie
was dressed, or at least had been dressed at breakfast
time, in a clean white frock, low shoes and white stock-
ings, although all now showed signs of strenuous usage.

Clutched to her breast as she ran up to her mother's side was "Susan Jemima," her one beloved possession and her doll. Behind Virgie came Sally Ann, her playmate, a slim, barefooted mulatto girl whose faded, gingham dress hung partly in tatters, halfway between her knees and ankles. In one of Sally Ann's hands, carried like a sword, was a pointed stick; in the other, a long piece of blue woodmoss from which dangled a bit of string.

"Oh, Mother," cried the small daughter of the Carys, as she came up flushed and excited, "what do you reckon Sally Ann and me have been playing out in the woods!"

"What, dear!" and Mrs. Cary's gentle hand went up to lift the hair back from her daughter's dampened forehead.

"*Blue Beard!*" cried Virgie, with rounded eyes.

"Blue Beard!" echoed her mother in astonishment at this childish freak of amusement. "Not really—on this hot day."

"Um, hum," nodded Virgie emphatically. "You know he—he—he was the terriblest old man that—that ever was. An' he had so many wifses that—"

"Say 'wives,' my darling. *Wives.*"

Sally Ann laughed and Virgie frowned.

"Well, I *thought* it was that, but Sally Ann's older'n me and she said 'wifses.'"

"Huh," grunted Sally Ann. "Don' make no differ'nce what you call 'em, des so he had 'em. Gor'n tell her."

"Well, you know, Mother, Blue Beard had such a bad

habit of killin' his wives that—that some of the ladies got so they—they almost didn't like to marry him!"

"Gracious, what a state of affairs," cried Mrs. Cary, in well feigned amazement at the timidity of the various Mrs. Blue Beards. "And then—"

"Well, the last time he got married to—to another one—her name was Mrs. Fatima. An'—an' I've been playin' *her*."

"And who played Blue Beard?"

"Sally Ann—an' she's just fine. Come here, Sally Ann, an' let's show her. Kneel down."

Clutching the piece of moss from Sally Ann, Virgie ran behind the girl and put her chubby arms around her neck. "This is his blue beard, Mother. Hold still, Sally Ann—*My lord*, I mean—till I get it tied in the right place."

"Be keerful, Miss Virgie," advised the colored girl. "You's a-ticklin' my nose. I'se gwine to sneeze ef yo' don't, and jes blow my beard all away."

"Oh, don't be such a baby," remonstrated the earnest Miss Virginia, with a correcting slap. "S'pose you were a man an' had to wear one all the time. Now! Stand up! Look, Mother!"

"I'm afraid of him already. He's so ferocious.

"Isn't he? Oh, won't *you* play with us, Mother? I'll—I'll let you be Mrs. Fatima." And then, as her mother's face showed signs of doubt as to her histrionic ability, "If you were *my* little girl, I'd do it in a minute."

"Very well, but before I do I must talk to Uncle Billy. You and Sally Ann wait here. Mrs. Fatima will be back with you very soon."

As Mrs. Cary walked toward the side of the house, a look of sadness and of worry shadowed her face.

War had seemed very thrilling, exciting, romantic— at first. But that was three long years ago. Mrs. Cary could still remember, as though it were yesterday, those early days when the boys in blue and the boys in gray had marched away to fight, each side for the cause it felt was right and just. As she walked toward the house she had only to listen to hear again in memory—

❋   ❋   ❋   ❋   ❋   ❋

Tara-tara!
From far away a faint fanfare of trumpets, borne on brazen wings from the distant clamor of the city's streets.
Tara-tara!
"What's that—a bugle?"
R-r-r-r-rum-dum!
"And that—a drum?"
Tramp—tramp—tramp—the rolling thunder of ten thousand feet.
War has been declared!
From North to South, the marching lines fill the land —a sea of men whose flashing bayonets glisten and glit- ter in the morning light. With steady step and even rank, with thrill of brass-lunged band and screaming fife the

regiments sweep by—in front, the officers on their dancing steeds—behind them, line after line of youthful
faces, chins in, chests out, the light of victory already
shining in their eyes.

In just this way the Nation's sons went forth to fight
in those first brave days of '61. Just so they marched out,
defiant, from South and North alike—with bright pen-
nons snapping in the breeze and bugles blowing gayly
and never a thought in any man's mind but that *his* side
would win and his own life be spared.

And every woman, too, waving cheerful farewell to
valiant lines of marching gray or sturdy ranks of blue,
had hoped the same for *her* side.

But in war there is always a reckoning to pay. Always
one contender driven to the wall, his cities turned to
ashes, his lands laid waste. Always one depleted side
which takes one last desperate stand in the sight of
blackened homes and outraged fields and fights on
through ever darkening days until the inevitable end
is come.

And the end of the Confederacy was now almost in
sight. Three years of fighting and the Seceding States
had been cut in twain, their armies widely separated by
the Union hosts. Advancing and retreating but always
fighting, month after month, year after year the men in
gray had come at last to the darkest, bitterest period of
it all—when the weakened South was slowly breaking
under the weight of her brother foes—when the two

greatest of the armies battled on Virginia soil—battled and passed to their final muster roll.

Of little heed to tell of the privations which the pivotal state of the Confederacy went through. If it were true that Virginia had been simply one vast arsenal where every inhabitant had unfailingly done his part in making war, it was also true that she had furnished many of its greatest battlefields—and at what a frightful cost.

Everywhere were the cruel signs of destruction and want—in scanty larder, patched, refurbished clothing, servantless homes—in dismantled outhouses, broken fences and neglected, brier-choked fields. Even the staples of life were fast diminishing for every man who could shoulder a gun had gone to fight with Lee and few animals were left and fewer slaves.

    ✻   ✻   ✻   ✻   ✻   ✻

Yet, for all the dismal outlook, Winter had passed without actual disaster to the Confederate arms and now that Spring had come the plantation home of the Herbert Carys, twenty miles below Richmond, had never had a fairer setting. White-pillared and stately the old Colonial mansion stood on one of the low, emerald hills which roll back lazily from the peaceful James. It was true that the flower beds had been trampled down to ruin by alien horse and heel, but the scent of the honeysuckle clinging to those shining pillars only seemed the sweeter for the loss, and whatever else the forager might take, he could not rob them of their gracious vista of hills and shimmering river.

For good reason the plantation was very silent on this warm spring morning. Where only a year before dozens of soft eyed Jerseys had ranged through the pastures and wood lots there was now no sound of tinkling bells —one after another the fine, blooded stock had been requisitioned by a sad faced quartermaster of the Army of Northern Virginia. And one by one the fat porkers who had muzzled greedily among the ears from the Cary bins and who ought to have gone into the smoke house had departed, squealing, to furnish bone and sinew with which to repel the invader. Saddest of all, the chicken coops down by the deserted Negro quarters were quite as empty as the once teeming cabins themselves. Poverty, grim and relentless, had caught the Carys in its iron hand and behind Poverty stood its far more frightening shadow—Starvation.

All this and more was in old Uncle Billy's gray, kinky head as he emerged from the woods below the house and came slowly up the driveway and he sat down on a bench under a tree to ruminate over the situation and inspect the feathered prize which he had lately acquired by certain, devious means known only to Uncle Billy. Wiping his forehead with his ragged sleeve and holding the bird up by its tied feet he regarded it with the eye of an expert, and the fatigue of one who has been sorely put to it in order to accomplish his purpose.

"It 'pears to me," said Uncle Billy, "dat des' when you needs 'em the mostest the chickens goes to roosting higher 'n' higher. Rooster—I wonder who you b'longs to. Um-*um!*" he murmured as he thoughtfully sounded the rooster's well developed chest through the feathers. "From de feelin' of you, my son, I 'spec' you was raise' by one er de ol'es' fam'lies what is!"

But Uncle Billy knew the fortunes of the Cary family far too well to mourn over the probable toughness of his booty, and as he rose up from the seat and meandered toward the kitchen, his old, wrinkled face broke into a broad smile of satisfaction over the surprise he had in store. "Well—after I done parbile you, I reckon Miss Hallie be mighty glad to see you. Yas, *seh!*"

But as Uncle Billy walked slowly along beside the hedge which shielded the house on one side he heard a sound which made him halt. A young Negro, coming from the rear, had dodged behind the hedge and was trying to keep out of his sight.

"Hi, dar! You, Jeems Henry!" shouted Uncle Billy, instantly suspicious of such maneuvers. "Come heh! Hear *me*! You come back heh!"

At this sudden command a young mulatto, hesitating, came through a break in the hedge and stood looking at him, sullen and silent. In his hands he carried a small

bundle done up in a colored handkerchief and on this guilty piece of baggage Uncle Billy's eye immediately fastened with an angry frown.

"Whar you gwine?" demanded Uncle Billy, with an accusing finger trembling at the bundle.

The younger man made no reply.

"Hear *me*?" the elder demanded again in rising tones of severity. "Ain't you got no tongue in yo' haid? Whar you gwine?"

Shifting from one foot to the other the younger man finally broke away from Uncle Billy's eye and tried to pass him by.

"Den *I'll* tell you whar you gwine," shouted Uncle Billy, furious at last. "You's runnin' 'way to de Yankees, dat's whar you gwine."

At this too truthful thrust Jeems Henry saw that further deceit would be futile and he faced Uncle Billy with sullen resentment.

"An' sposin' I *is*—wat den?"

"Den you's a thief," retorted Uncle Billy with dismayingly quick wit. "Dat's what you is—a *thief*."

"I *ain*' no thief," Jeems Henry refuted stubbornly, "*I* ain' stole nothin'."

"You is too," and Uncle Billy's forefinger began to shake in the other's face. "You's stealin' a *nigger*!"

"What dat?" and Jeems Henry's eyes opened wide with amazement. "What you talkin' 'bout?"

"Talkin' 'bout *you*," replied Uncle Billy, sharper than

ever. "Dey say a nigger's wuth a thousan' dollars. 'Cose *you* ain't wuth dat much," he said with utter disgust. "I put you down at a dollar and a quarter. But dat ain't de p'int," and he steadily advanced on the other till their faces were only a few inches apart. "It's dis. *You,* Jeems Henry, belongs to Mars' Herbert Cary an' Miss Hallie; an' when you runs 'way you's stealin'. *You's stealin' yo'sef!*"

"H'm!" sniffed Jeems Henry, now that the nature and extent of his crime were fully understood. "Ef I ain' wuth but a dollar an' a quarter, I suttenly ain' stealin' *much!*"

At this smart reply Uncle Billy's disgust overcame him completely and he tossed the rooster on the ground and clutched Jeems Henry by the arm.

"You mighty right, you ain't!" he shouted. "An' ef I was fo' years younger I'd take it outer yo' hide with a carriage whip. Hol' on dar," as Jeems Henry eluded his grasp and began to move away. "Which way you gwine? You hear me? Now den!"

"I gwine up de river," replied Jeems Henry, badgered at last into revealing his plan. Then, after a cautious look around,—"to Chickahominy Swamp," he added in lower tones.

Uncle Billy cocked his ears. Here was news indeed.

"Chickahominy, huh! So de Yankees is up dar, is dey? An' what you think you gwine to do when you git to 'em?"

"Wuck 'roun de camp," replied Jeems Henry with some vagueness.

"Doin' what?" was the relentless query.

"Blackin' de gent'men's boots—an'—an' gittin' paid fer it," Jeems Henry stammered in reply. "It's better'n being a slave, Unc' Billy," he added as he saw the sneer of contempt on the faithful old man's face. "An' ef you wan' sech a crazy ol' fool, you'd come along wid me, too."

At this combination of temptation and insult Uncle Billy's eyes narrowed with contempt and loathing. "Me?" he said, and a rigid arm pointed back at the house which had been for years his source of shelter and comfort. "Me leave Miss Hallie *now*? Right when she ain't got *nothin'*? Look heah, nigger; dog-gone yo' skin, I got a great min' for to mash yo' mouf. Yes, I *is* a slave. I b'longs to Mars Cary—an' I b'longed to his pa befo' him. Dey feed me and gimme de bes' dey got. Dey take care of me when I'm sick—an' dey take care of me when I'm well—an *I* gwine to stay right here. But you? You jes' go on wid de Yankees, an' black der boots. Dey'll free you," and Uncle Billy's voice rose in prophetic tones—"an you'll *keep on* blackin' boots! Go 'long now, you low-down, dollar-an-a-quarter nigger!" as Jeems Henry backed away. "Go 'long wid yo' *Yankee* marsters—and git yo' freedom an' a blackin' brush."

So engrossed were both the actors in this drama that

they failed to hear the sound of footsteps on the veranda, and it was so that the mistress of the manor found the would-be runaway and the old slave, glaring into each other's eyes and insulting one another volubly.

Mrs. Cary, with her workbasket on her arm, paused at the top of the steps and regarded the angry pair with well-bred surprise. She was a true daughter of the old time South, low voiced and gentle and quiet eyed. Like all those self-sacrificing women who willingly drank their war time poverty down to its bitter dregs, her light, summer dress was of the cheapest material, yet her deft fingers had fashioned it with art, from slightly opened neck where an old-fashioned brooch lay against her soft throat down to the dainty, spotless flounces lying above her petticoat of crinoline. And every gesture and graceful movement, even in this moment of shocked surprise, was that of one so secure in the possession of breeding and tranquil authority as to be exquisite in its simplicity.

Time might work its will upon the fortunes of the Carys, but nothing could alter the sweet self-possession of this proud but gentle mother.

At the sound of Uncle Billy's angry tones Mrs. Cary raised her voice.

"Why, Uncle Billy," she queried, with pained amazement. "What is going on here? What *is* the matter?"

"It's Jeems Henry; dat's what's de matter," said Uncle Billy, in defense of his agitation. "He's runnin' 'way to de Yankees."

Mrs. Cary stopped short for a moment and then came slowly down the steps.

"Oh, James," she said, unbelievingly. "Is this really true?"

Jeems Henry hung his head and dug at the gravel with his toe.

"I'm sorry," said Mrs. Cary, and the word held a world of painful thought—of self-accusation, of hopeless regret, of sorrow for one who could be so foolishly misguided. "I'm sorry not only for ourselves but for *you*. You know, I promised Mammy before she died that I would look after you—always."

Still Jeems Henry made no answer and old Uncle Billy saw fit to make a disclosure.

"He's gwine up to Chickahominy." Then to Jeems Henry he added something in low tones which made the young Negro's eyes roll wildly with fear. "Dey tells me dat der's *hants* and *ghoses* over dar. I hopes dey'll git you."

"Stop that!" commanded Mrs. Cary. "You know very well, Uncle Billy, there are no such things as ghosts."

"Nor'm I don't, Miss Hallie," responded Uncle Billy, sticking tenaciously to his point, because he could plainly see Jeems Henry wavering. " 'Twas jes las' night I hear one—moanin' 'roun de smoke house. An' ef I ain't mighty fur wrong, she was smellin' arfter Jeems Henry."

At this wild fabrication, the reason for which she nevertheless appreciated, Mrs. Cary had hard work to hold back a smile, although she promptly reassured the terrified Jeems Henry.

"There now—there—that will do. Nothing of that kind will trouble you, James; you may take my word for it. If you are quite determined to go I shall not try to keep you. But what have you in that bundle?"

"Hi! Hi! Dat's de way to talk!" interrupted Uncle Billy, excitedly foreseeing means to prevent Jeems Henry's departure. "What you got in yo' bundle?"

Jeems Henry lifted his anguished eyes and gazed truthfully at his mistress.

"I ain't got nothin'—what don't b'long to me, Miss Hallie."

"I don't mean that," Mrs. Cary responded kindly. "But you have a long tramp before you. Have you anything to eat?"

"Nor'm, I ain't," and Jeems Henry seemed disturbed.

"Then you'd better come around to the kitchen. We'll see what we can find."

At this unheard-of generosity, Uncle Billy's eyes opened widely and he exploded in remonstrance.

"Now, hol' on dar, Miss Hallie! Hol' on. You ain' got none too much fo' yo'se'f, d'out stuffin' dis yere six-bit rat hole wid waffies an' milasses."

"*William!*" commanded his mistress.

"Yas'm," was the meek response, and Uncle Billy subsided into silence.

With a sigh, Mrs. Cary turned away toward the house. "Well, James, are you coming?"

But Jeems Henry, completely abashed before this miracle of kindness which he did not deserve, decided that it was time for him to be a man.

"Thank you, Miss Hallie," he gulped, "but f'um now on I reckon I gwine take keer of myse'f."

Mrs. Cary, pausing on the bottom step, raised her eyes heavenward in a short prayer that children such as these might somehow be protected from themselves.

"Well, James," she said, when she saw there was nothing more to be done. "I hope you'll be happy and contented. If you are not—come back to us. Perhaps, when the war is over, you'll find things a little more—comfortable. Good-by, James," and she held out her hand.

But this last touch of gentleness was too much for the young mulatto. Although he made an obedient step forward, his feelings overcame him and with an audible snuffle and his hand over his eyes he retreated—then turned his back and plunged through the hedge.

Mrs. Cary sank down on the step and looked as if she, too, would like to cry.

Manfully, Uncle Billy came to her rescue. "Now don't you care, Miss Hallie. He wan' no 'count for plowin' no how."

"Oh, it isn't that, Uncle Billy," Mrs. Cary replied with a low cry of regret. "It isn't the actual loss of help, tho' we need it, goodness knows. But it makes me sad to see them leaving, one by one. They are such children and so helpless—without a master hand."

"Yas'm," agreed Uncle Billy readily. "An' de marster's han' ought to have a hick'ry stick in it fer *dat* nigger. Yas, bless Gawd. But you got *me*, Miss Hallie," he announced proudly. "*I* ain't runned away to de bluecoats yet."

"No, you dear old thing," Mrs. Cary cried with laughing relief, and her hand rested on his shoulder in a gentle caress. "I'd as soon think of the skies falling. It is just such faithful friends as you who help me to fight the best."

"Um?" said Uncle Billy promptly, not quite understanding.

"I mean a woman's battles, Uncle Billy—the *waiting* battles—that we fight alone." Mrs. Cary rose to her feet and turned sadly away.

"Yas'm," agreed Uncle Billy. "I dunno what yo' talkin' bout, but I spec' you's right. Yas'm."

"Dear Uncle Billy," repeated Mrs. Cary, while her eyes filled with tears. "The most truthful—the most *honest*—"

Mrs. Cary stopped and looked sharply at something lying on the ground beside the steps. Then she turned and swept the old man with an accusing glance which made him quail.

"*William!*" she said, in awful tones.

"Yas'm," replied Uncle Billy, feverishly.

"What's *that*?"

Uncle Billy immediately became the very picture of innocence and ignorance. He looked everywhere but at the helpless rooster.

"What's what?" he asked. "Aw, dat? Why—why, dat ain' nothin' 'tall, Miss Hallie. Dat's—dat's des a *rooster*. Yas'm."

Mrs. Cary came down from the steps and looked carefully at the unfamiliar bird. No fear that she would not recognize it if it were hers. "Whose is he?" she asked.

"You—you mean who he b'longs to?" queried Uncle Billy, fencing for time in which to prepare a quasi-truthful reply. "He—he don' b'long to *nobody*. He's his *own* rooster."

"William!" commanded Mrs. Cary, severely. "Look at me. *Where* did you get him?"

Here was a situation which Uncle Billy knew must be handled promptly, and he picked up the rooster and made an attempt to escape. "Down on de low grouns— dis mornin'. Dat's right," he said, as he saw dawning unbelief in his mistress' face. "Now you have to skuse me, Miss Hallie. I got my wuck to do."

"One moment, William," interposed Mrs. Cary, completely unconvinced. "You are sure he was on the low grounds?"

"Cose I is!" asseverated Uncle Billy, meanwhile backing farther away.

"What was he doing there?"
Uncle Billy stammered.

"He—he—he, he was trespassin', dat's what he was doin'—des natcherly trespassin'."

At this marvel of testimony, Mrs. Cary's lips relaxed in a smile and she warned him with an upraised finger.

"Be careful, Uncle Billy! Be careful."

"Yas, *mar'm*," chuckled the old man. "I *had* to be. I never would a-got him! Oh, I's tellin' de trufe, Miss Hallie. Dis here ol' sinner tooken flewed off a boat what was comin' up de river. Yas'm. And he sure was old enough to know right smart bettern dat."

"And you *saw* him fly off the boat?"

"Oh, yas'm. I seed him. I seed him," and Uncle Billy floundered for a moment, caught in his own trap. "Dat is, not wid my own eyes. But I see him settin' in de woods, lookin' dat lonesome and losted like, I felt real sorry for him. Yas'm," and to prove his deep sympathy for the unfortunate bird he stroked its breast lovingly.

Mrs. Cary turned away to hide her laughter. "How did you catch him?"

"How?" repeated Uncle Billy, while his ancient mind worked with unusual rapidity. "I got down on all fo' in the thick weeds, an' cluk like a hen. An' den ol' Mr. Rooster, he came 'long over to see ef I done laid an aig —an' I des reach right out an' take him home to de Lawd."

"Oh, Uncle Billy," his mistress laughed. "I'm afraid

you're incorrigible. It's a dreadful thing to doubt one's very dinner. Isn't it?"

"Yas'm. An' I was des 'bout to say ef you an' Miss Virgie kin worry down de white meat, maybe den dis here bird'll kinder git eben wid me when I tackle his drum sticks. Yas'm," and with a final chuckle of joy over his success the old man hobbled quickly away in the direction of the kitchen.

Mrs. Cary, still smiling, went back to play Mrs. Fatima to a dusky moss-covered Blue Beard.

"Oh, goody, goody, here is Mrs. Fatima again!" and Virgie's dancing feet seemed hardly to touch the ground. "Come on, Sally Ann. We can play it with mamma's keys."

"Wait dar! Whar'd I put my s'wode?" And Sally Ann snatched up her dangerous weapon and thrust it into a rope around her waist. "Now I'se ready fo' killin' folks."

"But we have to begin where Blue Beard goes away on a journey," Virgie cried. "Susan Jemima, you sit there on the bench and clap your hands. Get up, Mamma. Go ahead, Sally Ann!"

"Ooman," said Sally Ann, strutting up to her mistress and frowning terribly. "I'se gwine away fer a night an' a day. Dese yere is de keys to de castle."

"Yes, sir," was the meek response.

Sally Ann Blue Beard pointed to an imaginary door halfway between them and where Virgie sat on the steps, wriggling with delight. "You kin look in ev'ry room in de house—castle, I means—'cept in des dat one. Orn'estan me? *Des dat one!* But ef yo' looks in *dar*,—Gawd he'p you. I gwine cut yo' haid off," and the fearful sword whizzed threateningly through the air. "Fyarwell—fyarwell."

"Farewell, my lord," said Mrs. Cary, and then in a whisper, as Blue Beard stalked away to hide behind a tree. "What *do* we do now? *Quick!*"

"Now *I* come in," cried Virgie. "I'm 'Sister Anne' that looks for the horseman in the cloud of dust." And jumping up, the child managed to change the tones of her voice in a surprising manner.

"Good morning, fair sister. Blue Beard has gone away, and now we can look in his secret room."

"No, Sister Anne, no! I dare not," and Mrs. Fatima shrank back full of fear from the imaginary door. "Urge me no more. I am afraid."

"But, Mother," cried Virgie, with a little squeal of disappointment. "You *have* to. It's part of the play," and she led her up to the invisible door.

"Now look in—and when you look—drop the keys—an' we'll both scream."

Slowly the door seemed to open and, after an instant's terrified silence, both actresses screamed with complete success. Whereupon Mrs. Fatima dropped to her knees and Sister Anne hugged her tight.

"It's blood. It's the blood of his seven wives. O-o-o-e-e-e!"

A great roar sounded in their ears.

"Mercy! What's that?" cried the terrified Mrs. Fatima.

"It's Blue Beard. He's coming back," whereupon Virgie immediately left Mrs. Fatima to face her fate alone.

Having spent a night and a day behind the tree, Blue Beard now rushed upon the castle and roared for his wife.

"Greetings, my lord," said the trembling Mrs. Fatima with a low curtsey, "I hope you have enjoyed your journey."

"Ooman," demanded Blue Beard severely. "What make you look so pale?"

"I know not, sweet sir. Am I, then, so pale?"

"You is! What you be'n up to sence I be'n away? Ha! What I tole you? Look at de blood on dat key! False ooman, you done deceib' me. Down on yo' marrow bones an' prepyar to die!"

"Spare me, my lord. Spare me! I am so—"

It was just about this time that old Uncle Billy, with a bridle in one hand and a carriage whip in the other came slowly upon the scene. At the sight of Sally Ann apparently about to assault his mistress, the bridle dropped from his hand and with a tight clutch on the carriage whip he covered the intervening space at an amazing speed.

"Hi, dar! You li'l woolly haided imp! You tech Miss Hallie wid dat ar stick an' I bus' you wide open!"

"Oh, stop, Uncle Billy!" cried Virgie in dismay. "We're only having a play!"

"Maybe you is; but I lay ef I wrop my carriage whip roun' her laig, des oncet, she'll hop all de way to de river."

At this dismal prospect, which seemed much truer than the play, Sally Ann began to whimper loudly. "Miss Hallie, ef he stay here, I ain't gwine to play."

"Whar you git dem whiskers at?" demanded Uncle Billy.

"Hush up!" cried Virgie.

"I'm hushin'," said Uncle Billy, retreating.

Thus reassured Sally Ann continued:

"I gwine down stairs to git my dinner. When I come back, I sho' gwine kill you. Fyar you well," and Blue Beard, making a wide circle around the carriage whip, took himself off the scene.

"Now, Mother," Virgie announced, "I have to watch at the castle window," and she jumped up on the bench.

"Sister Anne; Sister Anne, do you see anybody coming?"

"No one, Fatima—nothing but a cloud of dust made by the wind."

"Look again, Sister Anne. Do you see anybody coming?"

"Oh, Fatima, Fatima. It's growing bigger."

"Dar now," interposed Uncle Billy. "She's seein' som'pin."

"Sister Anne! Sister Anne. And what do you see?"

"Dust! Dust! I see a horseman in a cloud of dust. Look! Look! He's coming this way." By this time Virgie's acting had taken on so close a resemblance to the real thing that both Mrs. Cary and Uncle Billy rose to their feet in wonder.

"He's jumped the *fence*," cried Virgie. "He's cutting across our fields! He sees me! He's waving his hat to me!" With the last words the child suddenly jumped down from the bench and ran through the opening in the hedge, leaving her mother gazing after her in sudden consternation.

"Praise de Lawd, Miss Hallie," gasped Uncle Billy. "You reckon she done brought somebody, sho' 'nuff? Hi! Hi! *I* hear sum'pin. It's a horse. Lan' er Glory! Hits *him*!"

Chapter Two

Round the corner of the hedge at a swift trot came a man in the uniform of an officer in the Confederate Army,—and Virgie was in his arms.

Mrs. Cary gave him one look and threw out her arms. "Herbert!"

The man on horseback let Virgie slide down and then dismounted like a flash, coming to her across the little space of lawn with his whole soul in his eyes. With his dear wife caught in his arms he could do nothing but kiss her and hold her as if he would never again let her go.

"Hallie," he breathed, "but it's good to see you again. It's *good.*" And so they stood for a long moment, husband and wife united after months of separation, after dangers and terrors and privations which had seemed as if they never would end.

Sally Ann was one of the first to interrupt, edging up

at the earliest opportunity with her beard in her hand. "How you does, Mars' Cary? How you fine yo'sef, seh?"

"Why, hullo, Sally Ann!" said Cary, and put out his hand. "What on earth is this thing?"

Virgie ran to his side and caught his hand in hers. "We were playing 'Blue Beard,' Daddy,—an' you came just like the brother."

"So you've been Blue Beard, have you, Sally Ann?— then I must have the pleasure of cutting you into ribbons." Herbert Cary's shining saber flashed half out of its scabbard and then, laughing, he slapped it back with a clank.

"Sally Ann," he announced, "I'm going to turn you into Sister Anne for a while. You run up to Miss Hallie's room and sit by the window where you can watch the road and woods. If you see anything—soldiers, I mean—"

"Oh, Herbert!" cried his wife in anguish.

"S-s-sh!" he whispered. "Go along, Sally Ann. If you see anyone at all report to me at once. Understand? Off with you!"

Uncle Billy now came forward in an effort to make his master's clothes more presentable.

"Heh, Mars' Cary, lemme brush you off, seh. You's fyar kivered."

"Look out, you old rascal," Cary laughed, as his wife backed away coughing before the cloud of fine white dust that rose under Uncle Billy's vigorous hands. "You're choking your mistress to death. Never mind the dust. I'll get it back in ten minutes."

Mrs. Cary clasped her hands together at her breast with a look of entreaty.

"Herbert! Must you go so soon?"

Her husband looked back at her with eyes dark with regret.

"Yes," he said briefly. "I'm on my way to Richmond. How many horses are there in the stable?"

"Two—only two," was the broken response, as his wife sank down disconsolate on a bench. "Belle and Lightfoot—we sold the others—I *had* to do it."

"Yes, I know, little woman. It couldn't be helped. Here, Billy! Take my horse and get Belle out of the stable. Lead them down to the swamp and hide them in the cedars. Then saddle Lightfoot—bring him here and give him some water and a measure of corn. Look sharp, Billy! Lively!"

In the face of danger to his master Uncle Billy's response was instant. "Yes, seh. Right away, seh," and he took Cary's lathered animal and made off for the stables at top speed.

Mrs. Cary looked up at her husband with a great fear written on her face.

"Why, Herbert dear. You—you don't mean to say that the Yankees are in the neighborhood?"

Immediately Cary was on the bench beside her with his arm around her, while Virgie climbed up on the other side.

"Now, come," he murmured, "be a brave little woman and don't be alarmed. It may be nothing after all. Only —there are several foraging parties—small ones, a few miles down the river. I've been dodging them all morning. If they come at all they won't trouble either you or Virgie."

"But *I'm* not afraid of them, Daddy-man," cried the small daughter, and she doubled up her fist ferociously. "Look at *that*."

"Aha! There's a brave little Rebel," her father cried as he swept her up in a hearty hug. "*You're* not afraid of them,—nor you either, God bless you," and his lips rested for a moment on his wife's soft cheek. "Only, you are apt to be a little too haughty. If they search the house for arms or stragglers, make no resistance. It's best."

"Yes, yes, I know," his wife cried out, "but you, dear, *you!* Why are you here? Why aren't you with your company?"

Cary looked away for a moment across the fields and down the slope towards the shimmering river. They were very beautiful—he wondered why he had not fully realized all that wife and child and home meant to him when he volunteered recently for a certain hazardous duty. He knew, too, how quickly his dear wife would know the full extent of the peril with which he felt himself surrounded. And so his reply was short and seemingly gruff, as many another man's has been under too heavy circumstances.

"Scouting duty. I've been on it for the past two months."

Mrs. Cary's hand went to her heart.

"A *scout,* Herbert! But, darling, why? It's so dangerous—so horrible—so—"

He put up his hand, with a forced smile, to check her, and broke in gayly.

"Ah, but think of the fun in it. It's like playing hide-and-go-seek with Virgie."

But his wife was not to be put off so lightly and she put her impelling hands on his arm.

Cary changed his tone. His voice deepened.

"They need me, dear," he said earnestly. "What does danger to one man mean when Dixie calls us all? And I'm doing work—good work. I've already given one battle to General Lee and now I have information that will give him another and a bigger one. Two nights ago I came through the Union lines. I . . ."

Mrs. Cary rose unsteadily to her feet.

"Through the Yankee lines! Oh, Herbert. *Not as a spy!*"

"A spy? Of course not. I hid in the woods all day, then climbed a tall pine tree and got the lay of their camp—the number of their guns—the disposition of forces and their lines of attack. Yesterday I had the wires at Drury's Bluff and started trouble. I'm on my way now to join my command, but I had a good excuse for coming home to hold you in my arms again, if only for a moment. You see, poor old Roger got a wound in his flank—from a stray bullet."

"A *stray* bullet?" asked Mrs. Cary, doubtfully.

"Yes," he smiled, for he had escaped it, "a stray bullet meant for *me*."

"But, Daddy," Virgie interrupted, "while you were up in the tree—"

A wild whoop broke off Virgie's question. Sally Ann was rushing down the steps, her eyes rolling up with excitement.

"Mars' Cary! Mars' Cary! Somebody comin' 'long de road!"

"Who? How many?" Cary demanded, springing up and running towards the gate that opened on the wagon road over the hills.

"Des' one," responded Sally Ann with naïve truthfulness. "Ol' Dr. Simmons. He drivin' by de gate in de buggy."

Mrs. Cary threw up her hands with a muffled cry of relief and laughter. "Oh, Sally! Sally!" she exclaimed, "you'll be the death of me."

"But Lor'! Miss Hallie," said Sally plaintively, "he *tole* me fer to tell him."

Cary, returning, waved Sally Ann back to her post. "That's right," he laughed. "You're a good sentry, Sally Ann. Go back and watch again. *Scoot!*"

"Herbert," and his wife stood before him. "Come into the house and let me give you something to eat."

For answer Cary gently imprisoned her face in his hands. "Honey, I can't," he said, his eyes grown sad again. "Just fix me up something—anything you can find. I'll munch it in the saddle."

For a moment their lips clung and then she stepped back with a broken sigh. "I'll do the best I can, but oh! how I wish it all were over and that we had you home again."

A spasm crossed the man's face. "It soon *will* be over, sweetheart. It soon *will* be."

His wife flung him a startled look. "You mean—Oh, Herbert! Isn't there a single hope—even the tiniest ray?"

Cary took her hands in his, looked into her eyes and his answer breathed the still unconquered spirit of the South. "There is always hope—as long as we have a man." Mrs. Cary went into the house, slowly, wearily, and Cary turned to Virgie.

"Well, little lady," her father said, resting his hand on Virgie's shining head. "Have you been taking good care of mother—and seeing that Uncle Billy does his plowing right?"

"Yes, sir," came the prompt response, "Susan Jemima an' me have been lookin' after everything—but we had to eat up General Butler!"

"General Butler," cried her father, astounded.

"Yes, Daddy—our lastest calf. We named him that 'cause one day when I was feedin' him with milk he nearly swallowed my silver spoon."

"Ha-ha," laughed the amused soldier, and swept her up in his arms. "If we could only get rid of all their generals as easy as that we'd promise not to eat again for a week. Everything else all right?"

"No, sir," said Virgie, dolefully. "All the niggers has runned away—all 'cept Uncle Billy and Sally Ann. Jeems Henry runned away this morning."

"The deuce he did! The young scamp!"

"He's gone to join the Yankees," Virgie continued.

"What's that?" and Cary sprang up to pace to and fro. "I wonder which way he went?"

"I don' know," whimpered Virgie forlornly. "I only wish I was a soldier with a big, sharp sword like yours— 'cause when the blue boys came I'd *stick* 'em in the stomach."

Mrs. Cary was coming down the steps now with a small package of food and in the roadway Uncle Billy stood feeding and watering his master's horse. In this bitterest of moments, when his own family had to be the ones to hurry him along his way, there had come another and greater danger—peril to those he loved.

"Tell me, dear," he said with his hand warm on his wife's soft shoulder. "Is it true that Jeems Henry ran away this morning?"

"Yes," she nodded. "I knew the poor boy meant to leave us sooner or later, so I made no effort to detain him."

"You did right," was the answer. "But which way did he go?"

"Up the river. To a Union camp on the Chickahominy."

"Chickahominy!" exclaimed Cary sharply, and bit his lips. "So that's the lay of the land, eh! I'm mighty glad you told me this. But still—" Cary's voice faded away under the weight of a sudden despair. What was the use of fighting forever against such fearful odds? What could they ever gain—save a little more honor— and at what dreadful cost?

"What makes you look so worried, Herbert?" his wife murmured, her nerves on edge again.

"Yes, it's true," the man said with a groan. "They're gradually closing in on us—surrounding Richmond."

"*Surrounding us?*" Mrs. Cary whispered, hardly believing her ears.

"Yes, it's true—all too true," the man burst out bitterly. "We can fight against thousands—and against tens of thousands but, darling, we can't fight half the world."

He sank down on the bench, one elbow on his crossed

knee, the other arm hanging listlessly by his side. His face grew lined and haggard. All the spirit, the indomitable courage of a moment ago had fled before the revelation that, try as they might, they could never conquer in this terribly unequal fight. Then he threw out his hand and began to speak, half to her and half to the unseen armies of his fellows.

"Our armies are exhausted. Dwindling day by day. We are drawing from the cradle and the grave. Old men—who can scarcely bear the weight of a musket on their shoulders: and boys—mere children—who are sacrificed under the blood-stained wheels. The best! The flower of our land! We are dumping them all into a big, red hopper. Feed! Feed! Always more feed for this greedy machine of war!"

Silently wife and daughter came to the man in his despair, as if to ward off some dark shape which hovered over him with brushing wings. Their arms went around him together.

"There, there, dear," he heard a soft voice whisper, "don't grow despondent. *Think!* Even though you've fought a losing fight it has been a glorious one—and God will not forget the Stars and Bars! Remember,— you still have us—who love you to the end—and fight your battles—on our knees."

Slowly the man looked up.

"Forgive me, honey," he murmured remorsefully. "You are right—and bravest, after all. It is you—you

women, who save us in the darkest hours. You—our
wives—our mothers—who wage a silent battle in the
lonely, broken homes. You give us love and pity—tenderness and tears—a flag of pride that turns defeat to
victory. The women of the South," he cried, and Herbert Cary doffed his hat before his wife, "the crutch
on which the staggering hope of Dixie leans!"

There came, then, the sound of hurrying footsteps.
Once more Sally Ann rushed from the house but this
time genuine danger was written plainly in her face.

"Mars' Cary! Mars' Cary! Dey's comin' dis time—
sho' 'nuff!"

"How many?" Cary cried, springing for the roadway
and his horse.

"Dey's comin' thu' de woods—an' Lawd Gawd, de
yearth is fyar blue wid 'em."

"Billy!" commanded Cary. "Take Lightfoot as fast
as you can down to the edge of the woods. Don't worry,
Hallie, they'll never catch me once I'm in the saddle."

He stooped and kissed her, then caught up Virgie for
a last hug, burying his worn face in her curls. "Good-
by, little one. Take good care of Mother. Good-by!"

With one last grasp his wife caught his hand. "Herbert! Which way do you go?"

"Across the river—to the Chesterfield side."

"But the Yankees came that way, too!"

"I'll circle around them. If they've left a guard at the
crossing I'll swim the river higher up." He slapped his

holster with his open hand. "Listen for three shots. If they come in quick succession—then I've crossed—I'm safe. If I only had a few men I'd stay, but alone, I can't —you know I can't. Good-by! God bless you." And in another moment he was in the saddle—had waved his hand—was gone.

Straining their eyes after him, as if they would somehow pierce the dark woods which hid his flight, mother and daughter stood as if turned to stone. Only Virgie, after a moment, waved her hand and sent her soft, childish prayer winging after him to save him from all harm. "Good-by, Daddy-man, good-by!"

Sally Ann, however, having seen the approaching danger with her own eyes, began to wring her hands and cry hysterically. "Aw, Miss Hallie, I so skeered!"

"Sally," cried Mrs. Cary, as the sound of hoofbeats thudding through the woods came unmistakably to her ears, "take Virgie with you instantly and run down through the grove to the old ice house. Hide there under the pine tags. Understand?"

But the Negro girl, ashen with terror, seemed incapable of flight.

"I skeered to go, Miss Hallie," she whimpered. "I wan' stay here wid you! Ou-ou!"

"But you can't, I tell you," her mistress answered, as the certainty of the girl's helplessness before a questioner flashed through her mind. "You'd tell everything."

"Oh, come on, you big baby," Virgie urged, pulling at Sally Ann's sleeve. "*I'll* take care of you." Then her eye fell on Susan Jemima lying neglected on the bench and she gave a faint scream at her heartlessness. "Goodness gracious, Mother," she cried, as, still holding on to Sally Ann, she ran and caught up her beloved doll. "I nearly forgot my child!"

With the clank of sabers and the sound of gruff commands already in her ears, Mrs. Cary turned peremptorily to Uncle Billy.

"Remember, William! If the Yankees ask for my husband *you haven't seen him!*"

"Nor'm, dat's right," was the prompt answer. "I dunno you eben got one. But you go in de house, Miss Hallie. Dat's de bes' way,—yas'm."

"Perhaps it *is* best," his mistress answered. "The longer we can detain them the better for Captain Cary. You'd better come in yourself."

"Yas'm," replied the faithful old man, although such action was farthest from his thoughts. "In des' a minnit. I'll be dar in des' a minnit."

But once his mistress had closed the door behind her Uncle Billy's plan of operations changed. Hurrying down the steps he plunged his arm under the porch and drew forth—a rusty ax. With his weapon over his shoulder he hastened up on the veranda and stood with his back against the door.

Chapter Three

The thudding feet came nearer. A bugle call—a rattling of accouterments and then, from the other side of the hedge, came a half dozen troopers in blue, led by a Sergeant with a red face and bloodshot eyes.

"This way, boys!" the Sergeant shouted, and at the sound of a harsh, never-forgotten voice Uncle Billy's grasp on his ax grew tighter. "*I* know the place—I've been here before. *We'll* get the liquor and silver while the Colonel is stealing the horses, eh?" Then his eyes fell on Uncle Billy and he greeted him with a yell of recognition. "Hello, you black old ape! Come down and show us where you buried the silver and the whisky. Oh, you won't? Then I'll come up and get you," and he lurched forward.

"Look here, white man," Uncle Billy shouted, lifting the rusty ax high in the air, "you stay whar you is. Ef you come up dem steps I'll split yo' ugly haid! I know

44

you, Jim Dudley," he cried. "Mars' Cary done give you *one* horse whippin', an' ef you hang aroun' here you'll get anudder one!"

Furious at the recollection of his shame of a few years back when he had been overseer on this same plantation, the Sergeant rushed up the steps and knocked the ax aside with his gun barrel. "Yes, he did whip me, burn him, and now I'll do the same for you." Seizing Uncle Billy by the throat he pushed him against the house.

Instantly the door swung open. Mrs. Cary, her head held high, her beautiful dark eyes blazing with wrath, stood on the threshold.

"Stop it!" she commanded in tones that brooked no disobedience even from a drunkard. "Let my servant go—instantly!"

Astounded at this sudden apparition the man shrank back for a moment, but almost as quickly regained his bluster.

"Ah-hah, the beautiful Mrs. Cary, eh! I'm glad to see you looking so well—and handsome."

The words might as well have been spoken to the wind for all the notice that the woman paid them. With only a gesture of mingled contempt and loathing she stepped to the railing and called to the grinning troopers below. "Who is in command here?"

To her horror only Dudley answered.

"*I* am," he said, triumphantly. He thrust a menacing

face close to hers and ordered her curtly. "And I'd just as soon have *you* get me a drink as the nigger. Come on, fine lady."

Intent on insulting this woman whose husband had once cut his back with a whip the man caught her by the arm and roughly tried to pull her to him. But before he could accomplish his purpose retribution fell on him with a heavy hand.

Through a gap in the hedge an officer at the head of a dozen troopers appeared. One look at the scene on the veranda and Lieutenant-Colonel Morrison, with a smothered cry, dashed up the steps.

"You beastly coward," and catching the drunkard by the collar he twisted him around and hurled him thudding and bumping down the steps. "Dudley, I ought to have you shot." He swept his arm out and gave voice to a ringing command. "Report to Lieutenant Harris— at once—*under arrest!* Corporal! Take his gun." He paused a moment as a brother of the man now under arrest stepped forward with a sullen face and obeyed orders. Running his glance over the line of faces, now suddenly vacant of expression, he whipped them mercilessly with his eye. "You men, too, will hear from me. Go to the stable and wait. Another piece of work like this and I'll have your coats cut off with a belt buckle! Clear out!"

Then he turned to the beautiful woman in white who stood only a few feet away, no longer timid but in entire possession of her faculties before what, she knew, might prove a greater danger than a drunkard.

"Madam," said the Union officer as he doffed his hat, "I couldn't apologize for this, no matter how hard I tried; but, believe me, I regret it—deeply."

In answer she slowly raised her heavy lidded eyes and gave him her first thrust—smoothly and deftly.

"No apology is demanded," she murmured in soft tones. "I was merely unfamiliar with the Union's method of attack."

"Attack!" he repeated, astounded, and stepped back.

"What else?" she asked, simply. "My home is overrun; my servant assaulted—by a drunken ruffian."

"The man will be punished," was the stern reply, "to the limit of my authority."

"He *should* be. We know him," the Southern woman said bitterly. "Before the war he was our overseer. He was cruel to the Negroes and my husband gave him a taste of his own discipline—with a riding whip!"

"Ah, I see," Morrison nodded. "But it is not always in an officer's power to control each individual in the service—especially at such a time. Yet I assure you on the part of the Union—and mine—that there was no intention of attack."

Mrs. Cary had chosen this moment in which to draw her visitor off the veranda and when she had successfully brought him to the foot of the steps she looked up in smiling sarcasm with another thrust.

"Oh! Then since your visit would seem a *social* one —how, may I serve you, sir?"

Morrison laughed lightly. This pretty cat could scratch.

"I'm afraid, dear madam, you are wrong again. My detachment is on foraging duty. It is not a pleasant task —but our army is in need of horses and supplies, and by the rules of war, I must take what I can find."

"Even by force?" came the quiet inquiry.

"Yes, even force," he answered, reddening. "With its proper limitations. I rob you, it is true, but by virtue of necessity. In return I can only offer, as I would to every other woman of the South, all courtesy and protection at my command," and Lieutenant-Colonel Morrison, for the second time, took off his hat.

The Southern woman swept him a curtsey filled with graceful mockery.

"I thank you. There is consolation—and even flattery —in being plundered by a gentleman." She made a short gesture which took in house, plantation and all the Cary possessions. "I regret sincerely that we have nothing left; yet I beg you—help yourself."

Colonel Morrison bit his lip, half in vexation and half in amusement. "At least you make my undertaking a difficult one, although I must admit, I hardly blame you." And then, with a quick, searching look, "Are there any rebels hidden in your house?"

"No," she answered.

"No wounded officers—or refugees of any kind?"

"None."

"You give me your word for this—your oath?"

The Southern woman's head went up and her eyes flashed. "I do," she said contemptuously and moved away.

"Thank you," was the grave reply, and he turned to dismiss his men. Then a thought struck him and he detained her with a gesture.

"Pardon me, but if it *was* true—if a brother or a father—was concealed in there—wouldn't your answer be the same?"

The answer that came proudly back did not amaze him. "I would try to protect them—yes! Even with a *perjury!*"

"Ah!" he said sharply. "Then, don't you see, you tie the hands of courtesy and *force* me to—to this invasion of your home. *Corporal!* Make a search of the house for hidden arms or stragglers and report to me. If any rebels are found—bring them out. Wait," he ordered, as the Corporal promptly started forward, "nothing else, *whatever*, must be taken or molested."

"One moment," commanded Mrs. Cary in her turn and beckoned to Uncle Billy who had been standing by in silence. "William! Conduct these soldiers through my house—and show them every courtesy. If the Colonel's orders are not obeyed, report to me."

"Yas'm," grinned Uncle Billy, with an opera bouffe salute. "Ev'ry molestashun I'se gwine report."

Morrison laughed outright. "I'm sorry you still have doubts of my honorable intentions. May—may my soldiers go in now? Thank you."

He walked away a few steps, then turned and looked at her where she sat on the bench demurely sewing. It occurred to him that she was *too* demure. Besides, he had discovered something.

"Er—it is true that I found your stable empty," he said, while his eyes probed hers, "but, curiously enough, it seems to have been recently occupied."

"Yes?" was the non-committal reply.

"Yes," he echoed, with a touch of iron in his voice. "And you can insure our leaving you more quickly if you will tell me where these horses have been hidden."

Mrs. Cary did not raise her eyes.

"Granted that we *had* them," she said, "I'm afraid I must trouble you to look for them. Otherwise there would be no sense in trying to protect my property."

"Right again," he acknowledged, but did not swerve from what he had to do. "Orderly," he commanded, "report to Lieutenant Harris at the stables and have him hunt the woods and swamp for hidden horses. Hurry! We must leave in half an hour."

As Morrison spoke his eye fell on the roadway and he started perceptibly. When he turned back to the woman on the bench it was with a sterner light in his eye.

"I also notice that a horse has recently been fed and watered in your carriage road. *Whose was he?*"

Again that smooth, soft voice with its languid evasions. "We have several neighbors, Colonel. They visit us at infrequent times."

"Undoubtedly," he conceded. "But do you usually feed their horses?"

She smiled faintly. "What little hospitality is ours extends to both man and beast."

"I can well believe it," he replied, for he saw to cross-examine this quick witted woman would be forever useless. "And in happier times I could wish it might extend—to me.

"Oh, I mean no offense," he interrupted as Mrs. Cary rose haughtily. "I only want you to believe that I'm sorry for this intrusion."

She raised her eyebrows faintly and sat down again. "And was that the reason why you asked about my neighbor's horse?"

"No," he said quickly, and as suddenly caught and held her eye. "There's a Rebel scout who has been giving us trouble—a handsome fellow riding a bay horse. I thought, perhaps, he might have passed this way."

If he had thought he would detect anything in her face he was once more mistaken.

"It is more than possible," Mrs. Cary remarked with a touch of weariness. "The road out there is a public one."

"And where does it lead to, may I ask?"

"That depends upon which way you are traveling—and which fork you take."

"Possibly. But suppose you were riding north. Wouldn't the right fork lead to Richmond—and the left swing around toward the river crossing?"

"As to that I must refer you to a more competent authority," she answered with a hint of some disclosure in her tones.

"Who?"

"Mr. Jefferson Davis," she replied and almost laughed outright as he turned away to hide his vexation. This was an easy game for her to play—and every moment she gained added to Herbert's safety. But if only she could hear those three shots from across the river.

"Well, Harris?" said Morrison as his Lieutenant strode up.

"I have to report, sir, that we've gotten what little hay and corn there was in the stables and are waiting for your orders."

"Very well," and Lieutenant-Colonel Morrison's incisive words rang mercilessly in the listening woman's ears. "Pick out the best shots you have among your men and send them at a gallop down this road to the river crossing. String them along the bank, dismount them and have them watch as they've never watched before. You understand? Now *hurry!*"

If ever a woman hated a man, or rather the crushing force he typified, then Herbert Cary's wife hated this clear headed, efficient Northerner, who was now discovering how he had been delayed and thwarted. Yet she had plenty of spirit left, for as Corporal Dudley and his file of troopers emerged from the house she stood up and caught Uncle Billy's eye.

"Well, Corporal?" asked Morrison.

"Well, William?" asked Mrs. Cary.

"It's all right, Miss Hallie," Uncle Billy grinned. "Dey ain't took nothin'—not a single thing."

"Thank you, William," said Mrs. Cary, having triumphed again. "And thank *you*, gentlemen." With a bow to Morrison she went superbly back to her seat under the trees. But as she went it took all her strength of will to keep from crying. Down the carriage road a squad of cavalry was galloping furiously towards the river. And still she had not heard the three shots.

"Now, then, Corporal, you found what?"

"Nothing, sir. We hunted from cellar to roof. No arms and no rebels."

"H'm," he mused. "Anything else?"

"Three bedrooms, sir. All in use."

"Three?" Colonel Morrison exclaimed. "Very well. That's all. I'll join you in a moment." Then he turned to Mrs. Cary, his face stern with resolve.

"Madam," he said crisply, "you are not alone on this plantation with only this old Negro. We are wasting time. I'm after a Rebel scout and *I want him*. Which way did he go?"

"I'm sorry, sir," she said, quite ready to play her game again. "But our Rebel scouts usually neglect to mention their precise intentions."

"Perhaps. If this one went at all. Is he still here?"

"I should imagine—*not*."

"Then he did go this way—to the river crossing?"

Once more he caught and held her eyes and thought he would read the truth in spite of anything she might say.

But while he looked he saw her strained face suddenly relax—saw the anxiety flee from her eyes—saw heart and soul take on new life. From far away across the river had come some faint popping sounds, regularly spaced —*three shots*.

"Ah!" he said, in wonder. "What is that?"

"It *sounds*," laughed Herbert Cary's wife, "like firing. But I think it is a friend of mine saluting me—from the safe side of the river. Good evening, Colonel," and she swept by him. She could go find Virgie now.

Just then came the sound of a horse, galloping. Up the road came a trooper, white with dust, his animal flecked with foam.

"For Colonel Morrison. Urgent," he rasped from a dry throat, as he thudded across the lawn and dismounted. "From headquarters," and he thrust out a dispatch, "I'm ordered to return with your detachment."

Snatching the dispatch from the man's hand Morrison ran his eye over it—then started visibly.

"Orderly! Report to Harris double-quick. Recall the men. Sound boots-and-saddles. Then bring my horse—*at once!* Any details?" he asked peremptorily of the courier.

"Big battle tomorrow," the man answered. "Two gunboats are reported coming up the river and a wing of the Rebel army is advancing from Petersburg. Every available detachment is ordered in. You are to reach camp before morning."

"All right. We'll be there." Then, as the bugle sounded, "Ride with us," he said, and strode over to where Mrs. Cary stood, arrested by the news.

"Madam, I must make you a rather hurried farewell —and a last apology. If ever we meet again, I hope the conditions may be happier—for you."

"I thank you, Colonel," the proud Southern woman said sincerely, with a curtsey. "Some day the 'rebel scout' may thank you also for me and mine." And with a smile that augured friendship when that brighter day should come she passed out of his sight among the trees.

For a moment he watched her, glad at least that the old Negro, her only protector, still guarded the house.

"Here, old man," he commanded, "go along with

your mistress and take care of her. I'll be the last to leave and see that nothing happens to the house."

"Yas, seh. Thank'e, seh," said old Uncle Billy, coming down. "If all of 'em was only lek you, seh—"

Uncle Billy suddenly turned and looked up at the house, his mouth open in consternation. With a cry of anguish he pointed to an upper window.

"Look what dey done done," he shrieked. "Aw, Gawd a'mighty! Look what dey done done!"

A cloud of smoke was rolling from the windows, shot through with yellow jets of flame. There was the sound of clumsy boots on the stairs and the door was thrown open. Dudley, escaped from arrest, ran out with a flaming pine torch in his hand.

"Halt!" cried Morrison, with raging anger. "Dudley! HALT!"

But Dudley knew that there would be little use in halting and so ran on until a big revolver barked behind him and he pitched heavily forward on his face. Morrison looked down on the prostrate form and his lips moved sadly, pityingly:

"And I promised her—protection!"

Chapter Four

I f all the memories of war, after the dear dead are buried, there is one that serves to bring the struggle back in all the intensity of its horrors—to stand both as a monument to those who bled and suffered and as a lonely sentinel mourning for the peace and plenty of the past —a blackened chimney.

Of all the houses, cabins, barns and cribs which had made up the home of the Carys a few short months ago nothing remained today but ashes and black ruin. Only one building had been left unburned and this, before the war, had been the cabin of an overseer. It had but two rooms, and a shallow attic, which was gained by means of an iron ladder reaching to a closely fitting scuttle in the ceiling. The larger room was furnished meagerly with a rough deal table, several common chairs, and a double-doored cupboard against the wall. In the deep, wide fireplace glowed a heap of raked-up embers, on which, suspended from an iron crane, a kettle simmered, sadly, as if in grief for her long-lost brother pots and pans. The plaster on the walls had broken away in patches, especially above the door, where the sunlight streamed through the gaping wound from a cannon shot. The door and window shutters were of heavy oak, swinging inward and fastening with bars; yet now they were open, and through them could be seen a dreary stretch of river bottom, withering beneath the rays of a July sun.

Beyond a distant fringe of trees the muddy James went murmuring down its muddy banks, where the blue cranes waited solemnly for the ebbing tide; where the crows cawed hoarsely in their busy, reeling flight, and the buzzards swung high above the marshes. Yet even in this waste of listless desolation came the echoed boom of heavy guns far down the river, where the "Rebs" and "Yanks" were pounding one another lazily.

From the woods which skirted the carriage road a man appeared—a thin, worn man, in a uniform of stained and tattered gray—a man who peered from right to left, as a hunted rabbit might, then darted across the road and plunged into the briery underbrush. Noiselessly he made his way to the now deserted cabin, creeping, crawling till he reached a point below an open window, then slowly raised himself and looked within.

"Virgie!" he whispered cautiously. "Virgie!"

No answer came. For a moment the man leaned dizzily against the windowsill, his eyes fast closed with a nameless dread, till he caught his grip again and entered the open door.

"Virgie!" he called, in a louder tone, moving swiftly but unsteadily toward the adjoining room. He flung its door open sharply, almost angrily; yet the name on his lips was tender, trembling, as he called: "Virgie! Virgie!"

In the loneliness of dread, he once more leaned for support against the wall, wondering, listening to the pounding of his heart, to the murmur of the muddy James, and the fall of a flake of plaster loosened by the dull reverberation of a distant gun; then suddenly his eye was caught by the kettle simmering on the fire, and he sighed in swift relief.

He wiped his brow with a ragged sleeve and went to where a water-bucket stood behind the door, knelt beside it, drinking deeply, gratefully, yet listening the while for unwonted sounds and watching the bend of the carriage road. His thirst appeased, he hunted vainly through the table drawer for balls and powder for the empty pistol at his hip; then, instinctively alert to some rustling sound outside, he crouched toward the adjoining room, slipped in, and softly closed the door.

From the sunlit world beyond the cabin walls rose the murmur of a childish song and Virgie came pattering in.

She had not changed greatly in stature in the past few

months, but there was a very noticeable decrease in the girth of her little arms and body, and her big dark eyes seemed the larger for the whiteness of her face. On her head she wore an old calico bonnet several sizes too large and the gingham dress which scarcely reached to her bare, brown knees would not have done, a few months ago, for even Sally Ann. In one hand Virgie carried a small tin bucket filled with berries; in the other she clutched a doll lovingly against her breast.

Not the old Susan Jemima, but a new Susan Jemima on whom an equal affection was being lavished even though she was strangely and wonderfully made. To the intimate view of the unimaginative, Susan Jemina was formed from the limb of a cedar tree, the forking branches being her arms and legs, her costume consisting of a piece of rag tied at the waist with a bit of string.

On a chair at the table Virgie set her doll, then laughed at the hopelessness of its breakfasting with any degree of comfort, or of ease.

"Why, Lord a-mercy, child, your chin don't come up to the table."

On the chair she placed a wooden box, perching the doll on top and taking a seat herself just opposite. She emptied the blackberries into a mutilated plate, brought from the cupboard a handful of toasted acorns, on which she poured boiling water, then set the concoction aside to steep.

"Now, Miss Susan Jemima," said Virgie, addressing

her vis-à-vis with the hospitable courtesy due to so great a lady, "we are goin' to have some breakfas'." She paused, in a shade of doubt, then smiled a faint apology: "It isn't very *much* of a breakfas', darlin', but we'll make believe it's waffles an' chicken an'—an' hot rolls an' batter-bread an'—an' everything." She rose to her little bare feet, holding her wisp of a skirt aside, and made a sweeping bow. "Allow me, Miss Jemima, to make you a mos' delicious cup of coffee."

And, while the little hostess prepared the meal, a man looked out from the partly open door behind her, with big dark eyes, which were like her own, yet blurred by a mist of pity and of love.

"Susan," said the hostess presently, "it's ready now, and we'll say grace; so don't you talk an' annoy your mother."

The tiny brown head was bowed. The tiny brown hands, with their berry-stained fingers, were placed on the table's edge; but Miss Susan Jemima sat bolt upright, though listening, it seemed, to the words of reverence falling from a mother-baby's lips:

"Lord, make us thankful for the blackberries an' the aco'n coffee an'—an' all our blessin's; but please, sir, sen' us somethin' that tastes jus' a little better—if you don't mind. Amen!"

And the man, who leaned against the door and watched, had also bowed his head. A pain was in his throat—and in his heart—a pain that gripped him, till two great tears rolled down his war-worn cheek and were lost in his straggling beard.

"Virgie!" he whispered hoarsely. "Virgie!"

She started at the sound and looked about her, wondering; then, as the name was called again, she slid from her chair and ran forward with a joyous cry:

"Why, Daddy! Is it you? Is—"

She stopped, for the man had placed a finger on his lip and was pointing to the door.

"Take a look down the road," he ordered, in a guarded voice; and, when she had reached a point commanding the danger zone, he asked, "See anybody?—soldiers?" She shook her head. "Hear anything?"

She stood for a moment listening, then ran to him, and sprang into his waiting arms.

"It's all right, Daddy! It's all right now!"

He raised her, strained her to his breast, his cheek against her own.

"My little girl!" he murmured between his kisses. "My little rebel!" And as she snuggled in his arms her berry-stained fingers clasped tightly about his neck, he asked her wistfully, "Did you miss me?—*awful* much?"

"Yes," she nodded, looking into his eyes. "Yes—in the night time—when the wind was talkin'; but, after while, when—— Why, Daddy!" He had staggered as he set her down, sinking into a chair and closing his eyes as he leaned on the table's edge. "You are hurt!" she cried. "I—I can see the blood!"

The wounded Southerner braced himself.

"No, dear, no," he strove to reassure her. "It isn't anything; only a little scratch—from a Yank—that tried to get me. But he didn't, though," the soldier added with a smile. "I'm just—tired."

The child regarded him in wondering awe, speaking in a half-breathed whisper:

"Did he—did he *shoot* at you?"

Her father nodded, with his hand on her tumbled hair.

"Yes, honey, I'm afraid he did; but I'm so used to it now I don't mind it any more. Get me a drink of water, will you?" As Virgie obeyed in silence, returning with the dripping gourd, the man went on: "I tried to get here yesterday; but I couldn't. They chased me when I came before—and now they're watching." He paused to sip at his draught of water, glancing toward the carriage road. "Big fight down the river. Listen! Can you hear the guns?"

"Yes, plain," she answered, tilting her tiny head. "An' las' night, when I went to bed, I could hear 'em—oh! ever so loud: Boom! Boom! Boom-boom! So I knelt up an' asked the Lord not to let any of 'em hit you."

Two arms, in their tattered gray, slipped round the child. He kissed her, in that strange, fierce passion of a man who has lost his mate, and his grief-torn love is magnified in the mite who reflects her image and her memory.

"Did you, honey?" he asked, with a trembling lip. "Well, I reckon that saved your daddy, for not one shell touched him—no, not one!" He kissed her again, and laughed, "And I tell you, Virgie, they were coming as thick as bees."

Once more he sipped at the grateful, cooling draught of water, when the child asked suddenly:

"How is Gen'ral Lee?"

Down came the gourd upon the table. The Southerner was on his feet, with a stiffened back; and his dusty slouch hat was in his hand.

"He's well; God bless him! Well!"

The tone was deep and tender, proud, but as reverent as the baby's prayer for her father's immunity from harm; yet the man who spoke sank back into his seat, closing his eyes and repeating slowly, sadly:

"He's well; God bless him! But he's tired, darling— mighty tired."

"Daddy," the soldier's daughter asked, "will you tell him somethin'—from me?"

"Yes, dear. What?"

"Tell him," said the child, with a thoughtful glance at Miss Susan Jemima across the table, "tell him, if he ever marches along this way, I'll come over to his tent and rub his head, like I do yours—if he'll let me—till he goes to sleep." She clasped her fingers and looked into her father's eyes, hopefully, appealingly. "Do you think he would, if—if I washed my hands—real clean?"

The Southerner bit his lip and tried to smile.

"Yes, honey, I know he would! And think! He sent a message—to *you*."

"Did he?" she asked, wide-eyed, flushed with happiness. "What did he say, Daddy? What?"

"He said," her father answered, taking her hands in his: "'She's a brave little soldier, to stay there all alone. Dixie and I are proud of her!'"

"Oh, Daddy, did he? Did he?"

"Yes, dear, yes," the soldier nodded; "his very words. And look!" From his boot leg he took a folded paper and spread it on his knee. "He wrote you a pass—to Richmond. Can you read it?"

Virgie leaned against her father's shoulder, studying the paper long and earnestly; then, presently looked up, with a note of grave but courteous hesitation in her tone:

"Well—he—well, the Gen'ral writes a awful bad hand, Daddy."

Her father laughed in genuine delight, vowing in his heart to tell his general and friend of this crushing criticism, if ever the fates of war permitted them to meet again.

"Dead right!" he agreed, with hearty promptness. "But come, I'll read it for you. Now then. Listen:

"HEADQUARTERS OF THE ARMY OF NORTHERN VA.

"Pass Virginia Cary and escort through all Confederate lines and give safe-conduct wherever possible.

"R. E. LEE, *General."*

There was silence for a moment, then Virgie looked up, with tears in her eyes and voice.

"An' he did that—for little *me*? Oh, Daddy, I love him so much, it—it makes me want to cry."

She hid her face on the coat of gray, and sobbed; while her father stroked her hair and answered soothingly, but in a tone of mourning reverie:

"So do we all, darling; big grown men, who have suffered, and are losing all they love. They are ragged—and wounded—hungry—and, oh, so tired! But, when they think of *him*, they draw up their belts another hole, and say, *'For General Lee!'* And then they can fight and fight and fight—till their hearts stop beating—and the god of battles writes them a bloody pass!"

Again he had risen to his feet. He was speaking proudly, in the reckless passion of the yet unconquered Southerner, only half-conscious of the tot who watched him, wondering. So she came to him quickly, taking his hand in both her own, and striving to bring him comfort from the fountain of her little mother-heart.

"Don't you worry, Daddy-man. We'll—we'll whip 'em yet."

"No, dear—no," he sighed, as he dropped into his seat. "We won't. It's hard enough on men; but harder still on children such as you." He turned to her gravely, earnestly: "Virgie, I had hoped to get you through to Richmond—today. But I can't. The Yankees have cut us off. They are up the river and down the river—and all around us. I've been nearly the whole night getting here; creeping through the woods—like an old Molly-cotton-tail—with the blue boys everywhere, waiting to get me if I showed my head."

"But they didn't, did they?" said Virgie, laughing at his reference to the wise old rabbit and feeling for the pockets of his shabby coat. "Did you—did you bring me anything?"

At her question the man cried out as if in pain, then reached for her in a wave of yearning tenderness.

"Listen, dear; I—I had a little bundle for you—of—of things to eat." He took her by the arms, and looked into her quaint, wise face. "And I was so glad I had it, darling, for you are thinner than you were." He paused to bite his lip, and continued haltingly, "There was bread in that bundle—and meat—real meat—and sugar —and tea."

Virgie released herself and clapped her hands.

"Oh, Daddy, where is it?" she asked him happily, once more reaching for the pocket. "'Cause I'm *so* hungry for somethin' good."

"Don't! Don't!" he cried, as he drew his coat away, roughly, fiercely, in the pain of unselfish suffering. "For Daddy's sake, don't!"

"Why, what is it, Daddy," she asked, in her shrillness of a child's alarm, her eyes on the widening stain of red above his waist. "Is—is it hurtin' you again? What is it, Daddy-man?"

"Your bundle," he answered, in the flat, dull tone of utter hopelessness. "I lost it, Virgie. I lost it."

"Oh," she said, with a quaver of disappointment, which she vainly strove to hide. "How did you do it?"

For a moment the man leaned limply against a chairback, hiding his eyes with one trembling hand; then he spoke in shamed apology:

"I—I couldn't help it, darling; because, you see, I hadn't any powder left; and I was coming through the woods—just as I told you—when the Yanks got sight of me." He smiled down at her bravely, striving to add a dash of comedy to his tragic plight. "And I tell you, Virgie, your old dad had to run like a turkey—wishing to the Lord he had wings, too."

Virgie did not smile in turn, and her father dropped back into his former tone, his pale lips setting in a straight, hard line.

"And then—the blue boy I was telling you about—when he shot at me, I must have stumbled, because, when I scrambled up, I—I couldn't see just right; so I ran and ran, thinking of you, darling, and wanting to

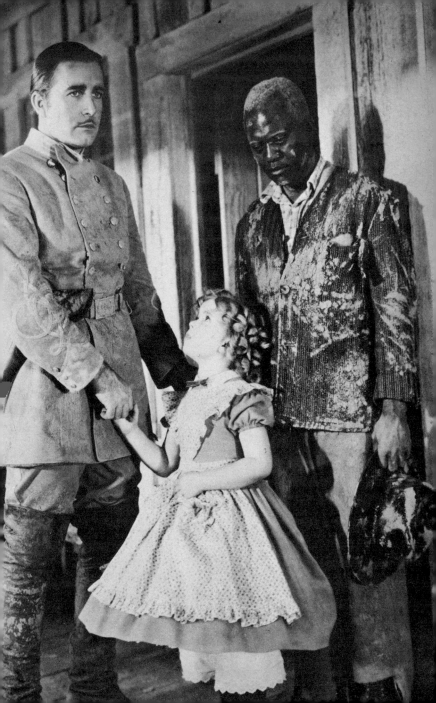

get to you before—well, before it was breakfast time. I had your bundle in my pocket; but when I fell—why, Virgie, don't you see?—I—I couldn't go back and find it." He paused to choke, then spoke between his teeth, in fury at a strength which had failed to breast a barrier of fate: "But I *would* have gone back, if I'd had any powder left. I *would* have! I would!"

A pitiful apology it was, from a man to a little child; a story told only in its hundredth part, for why should he give its untold horrors to a baby's ears? How could she understand that man-hunt in the early dawn? The fugitive—with an empty pistol on his hip—wading swamps and plunging through the tangled underbrush; alert and listening, darting from tree to tree where the woods were thin; crouching behind some fallen log to catch his laboring breath, then rising again to creep along his way. He did not tell of the racking pain in his weary legs, nor the protest of his pounding heart—the strain—the agony—the puffs of smoke that floated above the pines, and the ping of bullets whining through the trees. He did not tell of the ball that slid along his ribs, leaving a fiery, aching memory behind, as the man crashed down a clay bank, to lie for an instant in a crumpled heap, to rise and stumble on—not toward the haven of his own Confederate lines, but forward, to where a baby waited—through a dancing mist of red.

And so the soldier made his poor apology, turning

his head away to avoid a dreaded look in Virgie's big, reproachful eyes; then he added one more lashwelt to his shame:

"And now your poor old daddy is no more use to you. I come to my little girl with empty hands—with an empty gun—and an empty heart!"

He said it bitterly, in the self-accusing sorrow of his soul; and his courage, which had borne him through a hell of suffering, now broke; but only when a helper of the helpless failed. He laid his outflung arms across the table. He bowed his beaten head upon them and sobbed aloud, with sobs that shook him to his heels.

It was then that Virgie came to him again, a little daughter of the South, who, like a hundred thousand of her sisters, brought comfort in the blackest hours.

One tiny, weak arm was slipped about his neck. One tiny brown hand, with its berry-stained fingers, was run through his tangled hair, softly, tenderly, even as she longed to soothe the weary head of General Lee.

"Don't cry, Daddy-man," she murmured in his ear; "it's all right. *I* can eat the blackberries. They—they don't taste so *awful* good when you have 'em *all* the time; but *I* don't mind." She paused to kiss him, then tried once more to buoy his hope and hers. "We'll have jus' heaps of things when we get to Richmon'—jus' heaps —an' then—"

She stopped abruptly, lifting her head and listening, in the manner of a sheep dog scenting danger from afar.

Her father looked up sharply and gripped her hands.

"Virgie! You hear—*what*?"

"Horses! Oh, a lot of 'em! On the big road!"

It was true, for down the breeze came the faintly echoed thud of many hoofs and the clinking jingle of sabers against the riders' thighs. Virgie turned back from the open door.

"Why—why, they've turned into *our* road!" Her breath came fast, as she sank her voice to a faint, awed whisper, "Daddy—do you reckon it's—*Yankees*?"

"Yes," said her father, who had risen to his feet. "Morrison's cavalry! They won't hurt *you*; but I'll have to get to the woods again! Good-by, honey! Good-by!"

He kissed her hurriedly and started for the door, but shrank into the shadow at sight of a blue-clothed watcher sharply outlined on the crest of a distant rise. Escape was cut off, and the hunted soldier turned to Virgie in his need.

"Shut the door—quick!" She obeyed in silence. "Lock it!" She turned the rusty key, and waited.. "Now the windows! Hurry, but do it quietly."

She closed the clumsy shutters and set the heavy bars into their slots; then the man came forward, knelt down before her and took her hands.

"Listen, Virginia," he whispered earnestly; "don't you remember how your dear, dear mother—and I, too, darling—always told you never to tell a lie?"

"An' I haven't, Daddy-man," she protested, wondering. "'Deed, an' 'deed, I haven't. Why—"

"Yes, yes, I know," he interrupted hurriedly; "but now—*you must!*" As the child stepped backward and tried to draw away, he clasped her hands more tightly still. "But listen, dear; it's to save *me!* Don't you understand?—and it's *right!* When those men come, they mustn't find me. Say I *was* here, but I've gone. If they ask which way, tell them I went down past the spring— through the blackberry patch. Do you understand?— and can you remember?" She nodded gravely, and the Southerner folded her tightly in his arms. "Be a brave little rebel, honey—*for me!*"

He released her and began to mount the ladder leading to the scuttle in the ceiling; but halfway up he paused, as Virgie checked him with a solemn question:

"Daddy—would Gen'ral Lee want me to tell that lie?"

"Yes, dear," he answered slowly, thoughtfully; "this once! And, if ever you see him, ask him, and he'll tell you so himself. God help you, darling; it's for General Lee—and *you!*"

The littlest rebel sighed, as though a weight had been lifted from her mind, and she cocked her head at the sound of louder hoof-beats on the carriage road.

"All right, Daddy-man. I'll tell—a *whopper!*"

Chapter Five

The man crawled up through the scuttle hole and disappeared; then drew the ladder after him and closed the trap, while Virgie tiptoed to the table and slipped into a seat.

The cabin was now in semi-darkness, except for a shaft of sunlight entering through the jagged wound from the cannon-shot above the door; and it fell on the quaint, brown head of little Miss Virginia Cary, and the placid form of Susan Jemima, perching opposite, in serene contempt of the coming of a conquering host.

The jingling clank of sabers grew louder to the listeners' ears, through the rumble of pounding hoofs; a bugle's note came winnowing across the fields, and Virgie leaned forward with a confidential whisper to her doll:

"Susan Jemima, I wouldn't tell anybody else—no, not for anything—but I cert'n'y am awful scared!"

There came a scurrying rush, a command to halt, and a rustling, scraping noise of dismounting men; a pause, and the sharp, loud rap of a saber hilt against the door. Virgie breathed hard, but made no answer.

"Open up!" called a voice outside, but the little rebel closed her lips and sat staring at Susan Jemima across the table. A silence followed, short, yet filled with dread; then came a low-toned order and the crash of carbine butts on the stout oak door. For a time it resisted hopefully, then slowly its top sagged in, with a groaning, grating protest from its rusty hinges; it swayed, collapsed in a cloud of dust—and the enemy swept over it.

They came with a rush; in the lead an officer, a naked saber in his fist, followed by a squad of grim-faced troopers, each with his carbine cocked and ready for discharge. Yet, as suddenly as they had come, they halted now at the sight of a little lady, seated at table, eating berries, as calmly as though the dogs of war had never even growled.

A wondering silence followed, till broken by a piping voice, in grave but courteous reproof:

"I—I don't think you are very polite."

The officer in command was forced to smile.

"I'm sorry, my dear," he apologized; "but am afraid, this time, I can't quite help it." He glanced at the door of the adjoining room and turned to his waiting men, though speaking in an undertone: "He's in there, I guess.

Don't fire if you can help it—on account of the baby. Now then! Steady, boys! Advance!"

He led the way, six troopers following, while the rest remained behind to guard the cabin's open door. Virgie slowly turned her head, with eyes that watched the officer's every move; then presently she called:

"Hey, there! That's *my* room—an' don't you-all bother any of my things, either!"

This one command, at least, was implicitly obeyed, for in a moment the disappointed squad returned. The carbine butts were grounded; the troopers stood at orderly attention, while their officer stepped toward the table.

"What's your name, little monkey?"

Virgie raised her eyes in swift reproach.

"I don't like to be called a monkey. It—it isn't respectful."

The Union soldier laughed.

"O-ho! I see." He touched his hat and made her a sweeping bow. "A thousand pardons, Mademoiselle." He shot his sword into its scabbard, and laughed again. "Might I inquire as to what you are called by your—er —justly respectful relatives and friends?"

"Virgie," she answered simply.

"Ah," he approved, "and a very pretty name! Virgie what?"

"My whole name is Miss Virginia Houston Cary."

The soldier started, glanced at his troopers, then back to the child again:

"Is Herbert Cary your father?"

He waited for her answer, and got it, straight from a baby's shoulder:

"*Mister* Herbert Cary is—yes, sir."

The enemy smiled and made her another bow.

"I stand corrected. Where is your father now?"

Virgie hesitated.

"I—I don't know."

The voice of her inquisitor took on a sterner tone:

"Is he here?—hiding somewhere? Tell me!"

Her little heart was pounding, horribly, and the hot blood came into her cheeks; but she looked him squarely in the face, and lied—for General Lee:

"No, sir. Daddy *was* here—but he's gone away."

The enemy was looking at her, intently, and his handsome, piercing eyes grew most uncomfortable. She hung for an instant between success and sobbing failure, till a bubble from Mother Eve rose up in her youthful blood and burst into a spray of perfect feminine deceit. She did not try to add to her simple statement, but began to eat her berries, calmly, as though the subject were completely closed.

"Which way did he go?" the officer demanded, and she pointed with her spoon.

"Down by the spring—through the blackberry patch."

The soldier was half-convinced. He stood for a moment, looking at the floor, then asked her sharply, suddenly:

"If your father had gone, then why did you lock that door?"

She faltered, but only for an instant.

" 'Cause I thought you might be—Yankees."

"I see," he answered gently; "yes, I see." He turned away, but, even as he turned, his eye was caught by the double-doored cupboard against the wall. "What do you keep in there?" he asked; and the child smiled faintly, a trifle sadly, in reply:

"We *used* to keep things to eat—when we had any."

He noted her mild evasion, and pushed the point.

"What is in it now?"

"Tin pans."

"Anything else?"

"Er—yes, sir."

He caught his breath and stepped a little nearer, bending till his face was close to hers.

"What?"

"Colonel Mosby," declared the mite, with a most emphatic nod; "an' you better look out, too!"

The officer laughed as he turned to his grinning squad.

"Bright little youngster! Still, I think we'll have a look." He dropped his air of amusement, growing stern again. "Now, men! Ready!"

They swung into line and faced the cupboard, the muzzles of their carbines trained upon it, while their leader advanced, swung open the doors, and quickly stepped aside.

On the bottom shelf, as Virgie had declared, were a few disconsolate tin pans; yet tacked to the door was a picture print of Mosby—that dreaded guerrilla whose very name was a bugaboo in the Union lines.

The littlest rebel flung back her head and laughed.

"My, but you looked funny!" she cried to the somewhat disconcerted officer, pointing at him with her spoon. "If a mouse had jumped out, I reckon it would have scared you mos' to death."

The officer's cheeks flushed red, in spite of his every effort at control; nor was he assisted by the knowledge that his men were tittering behind his back. He turned upon them sharply.

"That will do," he said, and gave a brusque command: "Corporal, deploy your men and make a thorough search outside. Examine the ground around the spring—and report!"

"Yes, sir," returned Corporal Dudley saluting and dropping his hand across his mouth to choke off an exclamation of anger. Then he snarled at his men, to ease the pain of thwarted vengeance: "*'Tention! Right face! Forward! March!*"

The squad trooped out across the broken door, leaving their commanding officer alone with his rebel prisoner.

"Now, Virgie," he asked, in a kindly tone, though holding her eyes with his, "do you mean to tell me—cross your heart—that you are here, just by yourself?"

"Er—no, sir." As he opened his lips to speak, she pointed to her doll. "Me an' Susan Jemima."

"Well, that's a fact," he laughed. "Hanged if I'm not losing all my social polish." He gallantly removed his hat, bowed gravely to the cedar stick, and shook its hand. "Charmed to make your acquaintance, Miss Susan, believe me. My own name is Morrison—Lieutenant-Colonel Morrison—at your service." He turned to the little mother with a smile that showed a row of white and even teeth. "And now," he said, "since we are all informally introduced, suppose we have a quiet, comfortable chat." He paused, but she made no answer. "Well? Aren't you going to ask me to have some breakfast?"

Virgie cast a troubled gaze into the plate before her. "Er—no, sir."

"What? Why not?"

She faltered, and answered slowly:

"'Cause—'cause you're one of the damn Yankees."

"Oh! Oh! Oh!" exclaimed the soldier, shocked to hear a baby's lips profaned. "Little girls shouldn't use such words. Why, Virgie!"

She raised her eyes, clear, fearless, filled with vindi-
cating innocence.

"Well, it's your *name*, isn't it? *Everybody* calls you
that."

"Um—yes," he admitted, striving to check the twitch-
ing of his lips; "I suppose they do—south of Washington. But don't you know we are just like other people?"
She shook her head. "Oh, yes, we are. Why, *I* have a
little girl at home—not any bigger than you."

"Have you?" asked Virgie, her budding racial preju-
dice at war with youthful curiosity. "What's her name?"

"Gertrude," he answered softly, tenderly. "Gertrude
Morrison. Would you like to see her picture?"

"Yes," said the little rebel, and stepped across the
gulf which had lain between her and her enemy. "You
can sit down if you want to. Jus' put Susan Jemima on
the table."

"Thank you," returned her visitor, obeying instruc-
tions, seating himself and loosening the upper buttons
of his coat. On his neck, suspended by a chain, was a
silver locket containing the miniature of a plump and
pretty child. It had lain there since the war began,
through many a bivouac, many a weary march, and even
in the charge he could feel it tapping against his breast;
so now, as he held it out to Virgie, the father's hand was
trembling.

"There she is. My Gertrude—my little Gertrude."

Virgie leaned forward eagerly.

"Oh!" she said, in unaffected admiration. "She's *mighty* pretty. She's—" The child stopped suddenly, and raised her eyes. "An' she's fat, too. I reckon Gertrude gets lots to eat, doesn't she?"

"Why, yes," agreed the father, thinking of his comfortable Northern home; "of course. Don't you?"

Virgie weighed the question thoughtfully before she spoke.

"Sometimes—when Daddy gets through the lines and brings it to me."

The soldier started violently, wrenched back from the selfish dream of happiness that rose as he looked at the picture of his child.

"What! Is *that* why your father comes?"

"Yes, sir."

"I didn't know! I thought he came—"

He rose to his feet and turned away, his thoughts atumble, a pang of parental pity gnawing at his heart; then he wheeled and faced her, asking, with a break in his husky voice:

"And at other times—what do you eat, then?"

She made a quaint, depreciating gesture toward the appointments of her breakfast table.

"Blackberries—an'—an' coffee made out of aco'ns."

Again the troubled conqueror turned away.

"Oh, it's a shame!" he muttered between his teeth. "A wicked shame!"

He stood for a moment, silently, till Virgie spoke and jarred him with another confidence.

"My cousin Norris told me that the Yankees have bread every day; an' tea—an' milk—an' everything. *An' butter!*"

This last-named article of common diet was mentioned with an air of reverential awe; and, somehow, it hurt the well-fed Union officer far more than had she made some direct accusation against the invading armies of the North.

"Don't, Virgie—please," he murmured softly. "There are some things we just can't bear to listen to—even in times of war." He sighed and dropped into his former seat, striving gently to change the subject. "You have lived here—always?"

"Oh, no," she assured him, with a lift of her small, patrician brows. "*This* is the overseer's house. *Our* house used to be up on the hill, in the grove."

"*Used* to be—?"

"Yes, sir. But—but the Yankees burnt it up."

Morrison's fist came down on the table with a crash. He remembered now his raid of some months before upon this same plantation, so unfamiliar in its present neglected state. Again he looked into the fearless eyes of a Southern gentlewoman who mocked him while her lover husband swam the river and escaped. Again he saw the mansion wrapped in flame and smoke—the work of a drunken fiend in his own command. Yes, he

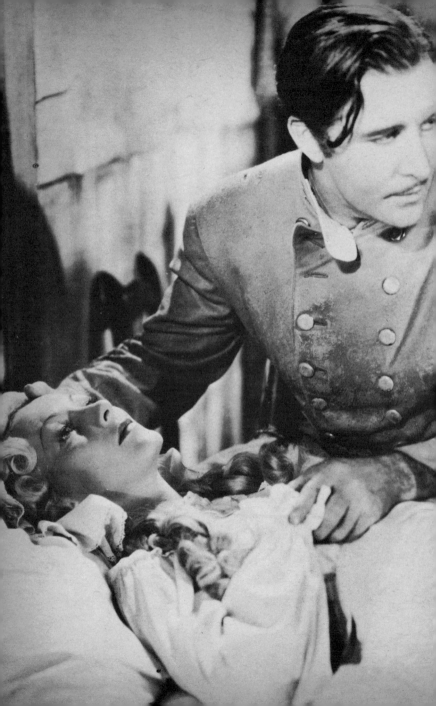

remembered now; too well; then he turned to the child and spoke:

"Tell me about it. Won't you?"

She nodded, wriggled from her chair, and stood beside the table.

"Oh, it was a long time ago—a month, maybe—an' they came after our horses. Mamma an' me were all by ourselves—'ceptin' Uncle Billy and Sally Ann. An' we were dreadful scared—an' we hid in the ice house."

She paused. Her listener had leaned his elbow on the table, his hand across his eyes.

"Yes, dear. Go on."

The child had been standing opposite, with Susan Jemima and the acorn-coffee pot between them; but gradually she began to edge a little nearer, till presently she stood beside him, fingering a shiny button on his coat.

"An' the blue boys ate up everything we had—an' took our corn. An' when they went away from our house, they—a man set it on fire. But another man got real mad with him, an'—an' shot him. *I* know, 'cause Uncle Billy put him in the ground." She paused, then sank her voice to a whisper of mysterious dread, "An'— *an' I saw him!*"

"Don't think about it, Virgie," begged Morrison, slipping his arm about the mite, and trying not to put his own beloved ones in the little rebel's place. "What happened then?"

"We came to live here," said Virgie; "but Mamma got sick. Oh, she got terrible sick—an' one night Daddy came through, and put her in the ground, too. But *he* says she's jus' asleep."

The soldier started. Mrs. Cary dead? This poor tot motherless? He drew the baby closer to him, stroking her hair, as her sleeping mother might have done, and waited for the rest.

"An' las' Friday, Sally Ann went away—I don't know where—an'—"

"What?" asked Morrison. "She left you here—all by yourself?"

"Yes, sir," said the child, with a careless laugh. "But *I* don't mind. Sally Ann was a triflin' nigger, anyhow. You see—"

"Wait a minute," he interrupted, "what became of the old colored man who—"

"Uncle Billy? Yes, sir. We sent him up to Richmond —to get some things, but he can't come back—the Yankees won't let him."

"Won't they?"

"No, sir. An' Daddy's been tryin' to get me up to Richmon', where my Aunt Margaret lives at, but he can't—'cause the Yankees are up the river an' down the river, an'—an' everywhere—an' he can't." She paused, as Morrison turned to her from his restless pacing up and down. "My, but you've got fine clo'es! Daddy's clo'es are all rags—with—with holes in 'em."

He could not answer. There was nothing for him to say, and Virgie scorched him with another question:

"What did you come after Daddy for?"

"Oh, not because I *wanted* to, little girl," he burst out harshly. "But you wouldn't understand." He had turned away, and was gazing through the open door, listening to the muttered wrath of the big black guns far down the river. "It's war! One of the hateful, pitiful things of war! I came because I had my orders."

"From your Gen'ral?"

He lowered his chin, regarding her in mild astonishment.

"Yes—my General."

"An' do you love *him*—like *I* love Gen'ral Lee?"

"Yes, dear," he answered earnestly; "of course."

He wondered again to see her turn away in sober thought, tracing lines on the dusty floor with one small brown toe; for the child was wrestling with a problem. If a soldier had orders from his general, as she herself might put it, "he was *bound* to come"; but still it was hard to reconcile such duty with the capture of her father. Therefore, she raised her tiny chin and resorted to tactics of a purely personal nature:

"An' didn't you know, if you hurt my daddy, I'd tell Uncle Fitz Lee on you?"

"No," the Yankee smiled. "Is he your uncle?"

The littlest rebel regarded him with a look of positive pity for his ignorance.

"He's *everybody's* uncle," she stated warmly. "An' if I was to tell him, he'd come right after you an'—an' lick the *stuffins* out of you."

The soldier laughed.

"My dear," he confided, with a dancing twinkle in his eye, "to tell you the honest truth, your Uncle Fitz has done it already—*several* times."

"Has he?" she cried, in rapturous delight. "Oh, *has* he?"

"He has," the enemy repeated, with vigor and conviction. "But suppose we shift our conversation to matters a shade more pleasant. Take you, for instance. You see—" He stopped abruptly, turning his head and listening with keen intentness. "What's that?" he asked.

"*I* didn't hear anything," said Virgie, breathing very fast; but she too had heard it—a sound above them, a scraping sound, as of someone lying flat along the rafters and shifting his position; and, while she spoke, a telltale bit of plaster fell, and broke as it struck the floor.

Morrison looked up, starting as he saw the outlines of the closely fitting scuttle, for the loft was so low and shallow that he had not suspected its presence from an outside view; but now he was certain of the fugitive's hiding-place. Virgie watched him, trembling, growing hot in the pit of her little stomach; yet, when he faced her, she looked him squarely in the eye, fighting one last battle for her daddy—as hopeless as the tottering cause of the Stars and Bars.

"You—you don't think he can fly, do you?"

"No, little Rebel," the soldier answered gently, sadly; "but there are other ways." He glanced at the table, measuring its height with the pitch of the ceiling, then turned to her again: "Is your father in that loft?" She made no answer, but began to back away. "Tell me the truth. Look at me!" Still no answer, and he took a step toward her, speaking sternly: "Do you hear me? *Look* at me!"

She tried; but her courage was oozing fast. She had done her best, but now it was more than the mite could stand; so she bit her lip to stop its quivering and turned her head away. For a moment the man stood, silent, wondering if it was possible that the child had been coached in a string of lies to trade upon his tenderness of heart; then he spoke, in a voice of mingled pity and reproach:

"And so you told me a story. And all the rest—is a story, too. Oh, Virgie! Virgie!"

"I didn't!" she cried, the big tears breaking out at last. "I didn't tell you stories! Only jus' a *little* one—for Daddy—an' Gen'ral Lee."

She was sobbing now, and the man looked down upon her in genuine compassion, his own eyes swimming at her childish grief, his soldier heart athrob and aching at the duty he must perform.

"I'm sorry, dear," he sighed, removing her doll and dragging the table across the floor to a point directly beneath the scuttle in the ceiling.

"What are you goin' to do?" she asked in terror, following as he moved. "Oh, what are you goin' to do?"

He did not reply. He could not; but when he placed a chair upon the table and prepared to mount, then Virgie understood.

"You shan't! You shan't!" she cried out shrilly. "He's my daddy—and you shan't."

She pulled at the table, and when he would have put her aside, as gently as he could, she attacked him fiercely, in a childish storm of passion, sobbing, striking at him with her puny fists. The soldier bowed his head and moved away.

"Oh, I can't! I can't!" he breathed, in conscience-stricken pain. "There *must* be some other way; and still—"

He stood irresolute, gazing through the open door, watching his men as they hunted for a fellow man; listening to the sounds that floated across the stricken fields—the calls of his troopers; the locusts in the sun-parched woods chanting their shrill, harsh litany of drought; but more insistent still came the muffled boom of the big black guns far down the muddy James. They called to him, these guns, in the hoarse-tongued majesty of war, bidding him forget himself, his love, his pity—all else, but the grim command to a marching host—a host that must reach its goal, though it marched on a road of human hearts.

The soldier set his teeth and turned to the little rebel, deciding on his course of action; best for her, best for the man who lay in the loft above, though now it must seem a brutal cruelty to both.

"Well, Virgie," he said, "since you haven't told me what I want to know, I'll have to take you—and give you to the Yankees."

. He stepped toward her swiftly and caught her by the wrist. She screamed in terror, fighting to break his hold, while the trap above them opened, and the head and shoulders of the Southerner appeared, his pistol held in his outstretched hand.

"Drop it, you hound!" he ordered fiercely. "Drop it!"

The Northerner released his captive, but stood un-moved as he looked into the pistol's muzzle and the blazing eyes of the cornered scout.

"I'm sorry," he said, in quiet dignity. "I'm very sorry; but I had to bring you out." He paused, then spoke again: "And you needn't bother about your gun. If you'd had any ammunition, our fire would have been returned, back yonder in the woods. The game's up, Cary. Come down!"

Chapter Six

The head and shoulders disappeared. A short pause followed, then the ladder came slowly down, and the Southerner descended, while Virgie crouched, a sobbing little heap, beside her doll. But when he reached the bottom rung, she rose to her feet and ran to meet him, weeping bitterly.

"Oh, Daddy, Daddy, I didn't do it right! I didn't do it right!"

She buried her head in his tattered coat, while he slipped an arm about her and tried to soothe a sorrow too great for such a tiny heart to bear.

"But you did do it right," he told her. "It was my fault. Mine! My leg got cramped, and I had to move." He stooped and kissed her. "It was *my* fault, honey; but you?—you did it *splendidly!*" He patted her tear-stained cheek, then turned to his captor, with a grim, hard smile of resignation to his fate. "Well, Colonel, you've had a long chase of it; but you've gotten my brush at last."

The Union soldier faced him, speaking earnestly:

"Captain Cary, you're a brave man—and one of the best scouts in the Confederate Army. I regret this happening—more than I can say." The Southerner shrugged his shoulders. His Northern captor asked: "Are you carrying dispatches?"

"No."

"Any other papers?—of any kind?" No answer came, and he added sternly: "It is quite useless to refuse. Give them to me."

He held out his hand, but his captive only looked him in the eyes; and the answer, though spoken in an undertone, held a world of quiet meaning:

"You can take it—*afterwards*."

The Federal officer bit his lip; and yet he could not, would not, be denied. His request became demand, backed by authority and the right of might, till Virgie broke in, in a piping voice of indignation:

"You can't have it! It's mine! My pass to Richmon'—from Gen'ral Lee."

Morrison turned slowly from the little rebel to the man.

"Is this true?" he asked.

The Southerner flushed, and for reply produced the rumpled paper from his boot leg, and handed it over without a word. The Northerner read it carefully.

"Pass Virginia Cary and escort through all Confederate lines and give safe-conduct wherever possible.

"R. E. LEE, *General."*

The reader crushed the paper in his fist, while his hand sank slowly to his side, then he raised his head and asked, in a voice which was strangely out of keeping with a Lieutenant-Colonel of the Union Cavalry:

"And who was to be her escort? You?"

The captive nodded, smiling his sad, grim smile; and the captor swallowed hard as he moved to the cabin door and stood listening to the muttered rumble of the river guns.

"I'm sorry, Cary," he whispered brokenly; "more sorry than you can understand."

For a long time no one spoke, then the Southerner went to Virgie, dropping his hand in tenderness on her tumbled hair.

"Just go into your room, honey; I want to talk to Colonel Morrison." She looked up at him doubtfully; but he added, with a reassuring smile: "It's all right, darling. I'll call you in just a minute."

Still Virgie seemed to hesitate. She shifted her doubting eyes toward the Union officer, turned, and obeyed in silence, closing the door of the adjoining room behind her. Then the two men faced each other, without the hampering presence of the child, each conscious of the coming tragedy that both, till now, had striven manfully to hide. The one moved forward toward a seat, staggering as he walked, and catching himself on the table's edge, while the other's hand went out to lend him aid; but the Southerner waved him off.

"Thank you," he said, as he sank into a chair. "I don't *want* help—from *you*!"

"Why not?" asked Morrison.

"Because," said Cary, in sullen anger, "I don't ask quarter, nor aid, from a man who frightens children."

The Northerner's chin went up; and when he replied his voice was trembling; not in passion, but with a deeper, finer something which had gripped his admiration for the courage of a child:

"And I wouldn't hurt a hair of her splendid little head!" He paused, then spoke again, more calmly: "You thought me a beast to frighten her; but don't you know it was the only thing to do? Otherwise my men might have had to shoot you—before her eyes." Cary made no answer, though now he understood; and Morrison went on: "It isn't easy for me to track a fellow creature down; to take him when he's wounded, practically unarmed, and turn him over to a firing squad. But it's war, my friend—one of the merciless realities of war—and you ought to know the meaning of its name."

"Yes, I know," returned the Southerner, with all the pent-up bitterness of a hopeless struggle and defeat; "it has taken three years to teach me—*and I know*! Look at me!" he cried, as he stood up in his rags and spread his arms. "Look at my country, swept as bare as a stubble field! You've whipped us, maybe, with your millions of money and your endless men, and now you are warring with the women and the children!" He turned his back and spoke in the deep intensity of scorn: "A fine thing, Colonel! And may you get your . . . reward!"

The Northerner set his lips in a thin, cold line; but curbed his wrath and answered the accusation quietly:

"There are two sides to the question, Cary; *but there must be one flag!*"

"Then fly your flag in justice!" the Southerner retorted hotly, wheeling on his enemy, with blazing eyes and with hands that shook in the stress of passion. "A while ago you called me a brave man and a good scout; and, because I'm both, your people have set a price on me. Five hundred dollars—alive or dead!" He laughed; a hoarse, harsh travesty of mirth, and added, with a lip that curled in withering contempt: "Alive or dead! A gentleman and a scout!—for just half the price of one good, sound slave! By Heaven, it makes me proud!"

Lieutenant-Colonel Morrison looked across the table at his prisoner, and answered gravely, yet with a touch of sternness in his military tone:

"You are more than a scout, Cary. You've carried dispatches, and intercepted ours; for both of which, if taken, you would have been a prisoner of war, no more. But you've entered our lines—not in a uniform of gray, *but blue*—and you've cost us the loss of two important battles."

"And had you done the same," returned the Southerner, "for you it would have meant promotion. I've served my cause as best I could; in the saddle or the rifle pit; in the woods, or creeping through your lines. If I've cost you a battle, my life is a puny price to pay, and I'd pay it without a sigh." He paused and sank into his seat. "For myself, I don't care much. I'm worn out, anyway; and I only wanted to get my little girl to Richmond." At the thought of Virgie his anger returned to him, and he once more staggered to his feet. "But you," he accused, "you've beaten a baby by the force of arms! You've run me to earth—and you've blocked her chance! It's Virgie you are fighting now—not me—yes, just as if you rode her down with a troop of horse! A fine thing, Colonel! For you, a brevet! For me, a firing squad! Well, call in your men and get it over!" Again he smiled; a grim, slow smile of bitterness and scorn. "Bravo, Colonel Morrison! Bravo! You add one other glory to your conquering sword—and, besides, you'll receive five hundred dollars in reward!"

The Northerner turned upon him fiercely, goaded at last to the breaking-point in a struggle as black and awful as the struggle of his brother-foe.

"Stop it, man!" he cried. "I order you to stop! It's duty!—not a miserable reward!" His cheeks were flaming; his muscles quivered, and his fists were clenched.

"Do you actually suppose," he asked, "that I'm proud of this? Do you think I'm wringing blood out of your heart and mine—for money?"

They faced each other, two crouching, snarling animals, the raw, primeval passions of their hearts released, each seeing through a mist of red; a mist that had risen up to roll across a mighty land and plunge its noblest sons into a bloody ruck of war.

They faced each other, silently; then slowly the features of the Southerner relaxed: His bitterness was laid aside. He spoke, in the soft, slow accent of his people—an accent so impossible to a trick of print or pen.

"I'm glad you feel that way; and maybe, after all, you're doing what you think is right. Yes—and I know it's hard." He stopped, then stepped a little nearer, timidly, as Virgie might have done. "Colonel," he said, scarce audibly, "I ask you just one thing; not for myself, but for her—for Virgie. Get the poor little tad through your lines, will you?—and—and don't let her know—about *me*."

His captor did not answer him in words, because of the pain that took him by the throat; but his hand went out, till it reached another hand that gripped it gratefully.

"Thank you, Morrison," said the prisoner simply. "If it wasn't war times—"

He choked, and said no more; yet silence proved more eloquent than human speech. They were men—brave men—and both were grateful; the one, because an enemy would keep his unspoken word; the other, because a doomed man understood.

Cary opened the door of his daughter's room and called to her. She came in quickly, a question in her big brown eyes.

"Daddy," she said, "you talked a mighty long time. It was a heap more than jus' a minute."

"Was it?" he asked, and forced a smile. "Well, you see, we had a lot to say." He seated himself and, drawing her between his knees, took both her hands. "Now listen, honey; I'm going away with this gentleman, and—" He stopped as she looked up doubtfully; then added a dash of gayety to his tender tone: "Oh, but he *invited* me. And think! He's coming back for *you*—to-day—to send you up to Richmond. Now, isn't that just fine?"

Virgie looked slowly from her father to the Union soldier, who stood with downcast eyes, his back to them.

"Daddy," she whispered, "he's a right good Yankee—isn't he?"

"Yes, dear," her father murmured sadly, and in yearning love for the baby he must leave behind; "yes—he's mighty good!"

He knelt and folded her in his arms, kissing her, over and over, while his hand went fluttering about her soft brown throat; then he wrenched himself away, but stood for a lingering instant more, his hands outstretched, atremble for a last and lingering touch, his heart a racing protest at the parting he must speak.

"Cary!"

It was Morrison who spoke, in mercy for the man; and once more Cary understood. He turned to cross the broken door; to face a firing squad in the hot, brown woods; to cross the gulf which stretched beyond the rumble of the guns and the snarling lip of war. But even as he turned, a baby's voice called out, in cheerful parting, which he himself had failed to speak:

"Good-by, Daddy-man. I'll see you up in Richmon'."

The eyes of the two men met and held, in the hardest moment of it all; for well they knew this hopeful prophecy could never be fulfilled. Morrison sighed and moved toward the door; but, from its threshold, he could see his troopers returning at a trot across the fields.

"Wait," he said to Cary; "I'd rather my men shouldn't know I've talked with you." He pointed to the scuttle in the ceiling. "Would you mind if I asked you to go back again? Hurry! They are coming."

The captured scout saluted, crossed to the ladder, and began to mount. At the top he paused to smile and blow a kiss to Virgie, then disappeared, drew up the ladder after him, and closed the trap.

The captor stood in silence, waiting for his men; yet, while he stood, the little rebel pattered to his side, slipping her hand in his confidingly.

"Mr. Yankee," she asked, and looked up into his face, "are you goin' to let Daddy come to Richmon', too?"

Morrison withdrew his hand from hers—withdrew it sharply—flung himself into a seat beside the table, and began to scribble on the back of Virgie's rumpled pass; while the child stood watching, trusting, with the simple trust of her little mother-heart.

In a moment or two, the troopers came hurrying in, with Corporal Dudley in the lead. He stood at attention, saluted his superior, and made his report of failure in the search.

"Nothing, sir. No tracks around the spring, and no traces of the fellow anywhere; but—" He stopped. His keen eyes marked the changed position of the table and followed upward. He saw the outlines of the scuttle above his head, and smiled. "But I'm glad to see that you've had better luck yourself."

"Yes, Corporal," said Morrison, with a sharp return of his military tone, "I think I've found the fox's hole at last." He rose and gave his orders briskly. "Push that table forward!—there!—below the trap! Two of you get on it!" He turned to the Corporal, while he himself climbed up and stood beside his men. "Light that candle and pass it up to me!" The orders were obeyed. "Now, boys, boost me!—and we'll have him out."

They raised him, till he pushed the trap aside and thrust his head and shoulders through the opening.

From below they could see him as he waved the lighted candle to and fro, and presently they heard his voice, that sounded deep and muffled in the shallow loft:

"All right, boys! You can let me down."

He slid to the table and sprang lightly to the floor, facing his troopers with a smile, half-humorous, half in seeming disappointment, as he glanced at Virgie.

"I'm afraid the little rebel's right again. *He isn't there!*"

"Oh!" cried Virgie, then clapped her hands across her mouth, while the troopers slowly looked from her into the level eyes of their commanding officer. He stood before them, straight and tall, a soldier, every inch of him; and they knew that Lieutenant-Colonel Morrison was lying like a gentleman. They knew that their chief was staking the name and title of an honorable soldier against the higher, grander title of "a man."

Only Corporal Dudley stood disconcerted at the startling statement, but as there was no help for it he could only strangle an oath and give the order to pass out.

"*'Tention! Right face! Forward! March!*"

They mounted and rode a rod or two away, awaiting orders; while Morrison stood silently and watched them go. He, too—like Virgie—had wrestled with a problem, and it stirred him to the depths. As a trooper must obey, so also must an officer obey a higher will; yes, even as a slave in iron manacles. The master of war had made his laws; and a servant broke them, knowingly. A captured scout was a prisoner, no more; a spy must hang, or fall before the volley of a firing squad. No matter for his bravery; no matter for the faithful service to his cause, the man must die! The glory was for another; for one who waved a flag on the spine of a bloody trench; a trench which his brothers stormed—and gave the blood. No matter that a spy had made this triumph possible. He had worn a uniform which was not his own—and the dog must die!

So ruled the god of warfare; still, did war prescribe disgrace and death for all? If Cary had crept through the Union lines, to reach the side of a helpless little one —*yes, even in a coat of blue*—would the Great Tribunal count his deed accursed? Should fearless human love reap no reward beyond the crashing epitaph of a firing squad, and the powder smoke that drifted with the passing of a soul?

"No! No!" breathed Morrison. "In God's name, give the man his chance!"

He straightened his back and smiled. He took from the table a rumpled paper and turned to the littlest factor in the great Rebellion.

"Here, Virgie! Here's your pass to Richmond—for you and your escort—through the Federal lines."

She came to him slowly, wondering; her tiny body

quivering with suppressed excitement, her voice a whispering caress:

"Do you mean for—for Daddy, too?"

"Yes, you little rebel!" he answered, choking as he laughed; "but I'm terribly afraid you'll have to pay me —with a kiss."

She sprang into his waiting arms, and kissed him as he raised her up; but when he would have set her down, her little brown hands, with their berry-stained fingers, clung tightly about his neck.

"Wait! Wait!" she cried. "Here's another one—for Gertrude! Tell her it's from Virgie! An' tell her I sent it, 'cause her daddy is jus' the best damn Yankee that ever was!"

The trap above had opened, and the head and shoulders of the Southerner appeared; while Morrison looked up and spoke in parting:

"It's all right, Cary. I only ask a soldier's pledge that you take your little girl to Richmond—nothing more. In passing through our lines, whatever you see or hear —*forget!*"

A sacred trust it was, of man to man, one brother to another; and Morrison knew that Herbert Cary would pass through the very center of the Federal lines, as a *father*, not a spy.

The Southerner tried to speak his gratitude, but the words refused to come; so he stretched one trembling hand toward his enemy of war, and eased his heart in a sobbing, broken call:

"Morrison! Some day it will all—be over!"

. . . .

In the cabin's doorway stood Virgie and her father, hand in hand. They watched a lonely swallow as it dipped across the desolate, unfurrowed field. They listened to the distant beat of many hoofs on the river road and the far, faint clink of sabers on the riders' thighs; and when the sounds were lost to the listeners at last, the notes of a bugle came whispering back to them, floating, dipping, even as the swallow dipped across the unfurrowed fields.

But still the two stood lingering in the doorway, hand in hand. The muddy James took up his murmuring song again; the locusts chanted in the hot, brown woods to the basso growl of the big, black guns far down the river.

A sad, sad song it was; yet on its echoes seemed to ride a haunting, hopeful memory of the rebel's broken call, "Some day it will all be over!"

And so the guns growled on, slow, sullen, thundering forth the battle-call of a still unconquered enmity; but only that peace might walk "some day" in the path of the shrieking shells.

Chapter Seven

It was afternoon and over on the eastern side of the James where the old Turnpike leads up over the rolling hills to Richmond the sun was pouring down a flood of heat. The 'pike was ankle deep with dust and the fine, white powder, churned into floury softness by artillery and the myriad iron heels of war, had settled down on roadside bush and tree and vine till all the sweet green of summer hung its head under the hot weight and longed for a cooling shower which would wash it clean.

In fairer times the Pike had been an active thorough-fare for the plantations and hundreds of smaller truck farms which fed the capitol, but of late months nearly all this traffic had disappeared. For the days of the Confederacy were drawing slowly but none the less surely to a close.

Inside the breastworks and far flung fortifications which encompassed Richmond the flower of the rebel arms, the Army of Northern Virginia, lay like a rat caught in a trap. On three sides, north, east and south, the Army of the Potomac under Grant beleaguered the city while the tireless Sheridan, with that lately developed arm of the Federals, the cavalry, raided right and left and struck hard blows at the crumbling cause where they were least expected. Yet in this same dark hour there had been a ray of light. Once the Confederacy had come within hairbreadth of overwhelming success, for Early's hard riding troopers had made a dash for Washington but a few weeks before and, with the prize almost in their grasp, had only been turned back by a great force which the grim, watchful Grant suddenly threw in between their guns and the gleaming dome of the nation's capitol.

But even this small success was not for long for when Early, crossing over into the luscious valley of the Shenandoah, began to scourge it with his hosts and threaten a raid into Pennsylvania, Sheridan broke loose from the restriction of telegraph wires and followed him to the death and finally broke the back of the great raid with his mad gallop from Winchester.

Meanwhile around Richmond, Lee and Grant, a circle within a circle, were constantly feeling each other out, shifting their troops from point to point in attack and defense,—for all the world like two fighting dogs hunting for an opening in the fence. And all the time the grim, quiet man in blue kept contracting his lines around the wonderful tactician in gray until the whole world came to know that unless Lee could break through the gap to the southwest the end of the war was plainly in sight.

And so it happened that on this hot July day the only sign of life on the 'pike was a small cloud of dust which drifted lazily in the wake of two people who passed along the road on foot.

One of the two was a tired, gaunt man in a ragged uniform of gray who stared up the long, hot road ahead of him with eyes in which there was, in spite of every discouragement, the light of a certain firm resolve.

The other of the two was a child with bare, brown legs and tattered gingham dress who limped painfully along beside the man, her sunny hair in a tangle half across her pinched and weary little face.

At a faint sigh of exhaustion from the child the man looked down, gathered her up in his arms and perched her on his shoulder. Then he plodded on again, a prey to weariness and hunger. The turning point in Herbert Cary's life had come. Thanks to a generous enemy; Virgie and he were now reasonably sure of food if once they could reach the Confederate lines; but as for himself, with the woman he had loved asleep forever beneath the pines, the future could only be an unending, barren stretch of gray.

Then, almost as quickly, recollection of his duty towards her whom he carried in his arms came to him and he raged at himself for his moment of selfish discouragement. Spurred on by the necessity of gaining a point of safety for his child he began to calculate the distance yet to be covered and their chances of gaining friendly lines before encountering scouting parties of Federals. Behind him, a few miles south on the other bank of the James at Light House Point, Sheridan was in camp with two brigades and Cary knew this fast riding, hard striking cavalryman too well not to suspect that the country, even in front of him, was alive with Union men. There was the pass which Morrison had given him, of course, but the worth of a pass in war time often depends more on him who receives it than on the signature.

But all those things, even food, would have to wait for a while because he was consumed with thirst and must find water before he went another mile forward.

A tired sigh from Virgie caught his ear and he stopped by a stone wall and let her get down from his shoulder. The child stood up on the broad, flat stones and then gave a little cry of pain. She raised one foot up and nursed it against her dusty, brown leg, meanwhile clutching her doll closer to her neck.

"It's all right, honey; be a brave little girl," her father said consolingly. "There's a spring along here somewhere and we can look after that poor little foot. Ah, there it is," he cried, as he caught sight of a big rock behind a stone wall with a seepage of water under it among some trees at one side. "Just sit still a minute—till I rest —and then we'll have a look." He leaned back against the wall and closed his eyes to shut out the dizziness with which exhaustion and hunger filled his aching head.

The child watched him anxiously for a moment and then put a soft little hand on his shoulder:

"Are you *so* tired, Daddy-man?"

"Yes, dear," he answered with a faint smile as he opened his eyes. "I had to catch my breath, but I'm really all right. Now then, we'll call in the hospital corps."

Virgie slipped down and sat on the top of the wall with her foot in her hand, rocking to and fro, but bravely saying nothing until her father's eye caught the look of pain on her pinched face.

"Does it hurt you much, dear?" he asked.

"Yes, sir. It—it hurts like the mischief," answered Virgie in a small voice. "It keeps jumping up and down."

"Little woman, that's too bad," he said with a consoling pat on the head which seemed to take most of the pain away. "But after we bathe it and tie it up it will feel better."

Kneeling beside the spring he took off his campaign hat of felt and dipped it full of clear, cold water.

"Wow!" cried Virgie suddenly in the interval and she slapped her leg with a resounding whack. "There are 'skeeters roun' this place. One of 'em bit me—an old *he* one. Jiminy!"

"Did he?" asked her father, smiling as he came back with the hat. "Well, honey, there are much worse things in this world than those little fellows and if you don't complain any more than that you're going to be a very happy lady when you grow up."

"Like Mamma?" asked the little tot, with a thoughtful face.

"Just like Mamma," the man repeated. "The loveliest —the bravest—and the *best*." He wavered a little on his feet and the hat threatened to slip through his fingers, but his daughter's great, dark eyes were steady on his and, curiously enough, he seemed to draw strength to pull himself together.

"And now, let's see. We'll have to get the grime off first. Just dip the little wounded soldier in."

"What! My foot in your hat!" protested Virgie with a little scream. "Oh, you poor daddy!"

"Why, that's all right, honey," he laughed, pleased at her daintiness. "That hat's an old veteran. He don't mind anything. So—souse her in.

"There—easy now—*easy*," as she threatened to capsize this curious basin. "Big toe first.

"Yes, I know it's cold," he laughed as the water stung

the broken skin and made her twitch involuntarily, "but bathing will do it good. I just know it feels better already—doesn't it?"

"Yes, sir," answered Virgie meekly, "only—it jumps up and down harder than ever. But of course I know it must be getting better."

"Good! What did I tell you? Now let Daddy look."

He lifted her foot up tenderly and examined it with care. "My, my!" he murmured. "You poor little soldier. If I hadn't looked around that time I expect you'd been willing to walk all the way to Richmond on a foot that would make a whole regiment straggle. Just see where you've cut it—right under the second little piggie. We'll have to tie it right up and keep the bothersome old dust from getting in. By morning you'll hardly feel it."

With a soldier's readiness he opened his coat and began to tear a strip from his shirt from which to make a bandage. But his small daughter interrupted him with a vigorous protest.

"Wait!" she cried, with a face full of alarm at the willful destruction of his garment. "Don't do that. Here! You can take it off my petticoat."

"*That* petticoat," her father laughed, with the first real mirth she had heard for many weeks. "That poor little petticoat wouldn't make an arm bandage for Susan Jemima. Now—up with your hoofie and let's play I'm a surgeon and you're a brave soldier who has fought in every battle since we first made the Yanks skedaddle at Bull Run."

With the painful foot securely bandaged the little girl gave herself up to thought, emerging from her study at last to ask what was an all-important question.

"Daddy—"

"Yes?"

"Do you reckon, by the time the war is over, we could call Susan Jemima a vet'ran?"

"I should say we could," the father agreed heartily, without the symptom of a smile. "Hasn't she grown bald in the service? And hasn't she almost lost an arm—or is it a leg I see dangling so terribly? I'll tell you what we'll do! We'll give her an honorable discharge—and decorate her. How's that?"

"Oh, fine!" she cried, clapping her hands with delight at the fantasy. "And we'll get that Yankee man to write her a pass just like mine. Do you hear that, Cap'n Susan," she crooned to the doll, unconscious of the convulsion of silent amusement beside her. "When we get to Richmon'—if we ever *do* get there—I'm going to make you a uniform!"

Then she turned to her father with a little sigh, for the miles seemed very long.

"How far *is* it to Richmon', Daddy-man?" she said.

"Just about twelve miles," her father answered. "But they're real old country miles, I'm sorry to say."

"Can we get to it tonight?"

The simple little question made the man's heart ache. What wouldn't he give for an hour of Roger once more —or Belle—or Lightfoot! Anything—even one of the old plantation mules would do if he could only perch her up on its back and take her into Richmond like a lady.

"No, dear, not tonight," he sighed. "We've come a long way and we're both tired. So when it gets dark we'll curl up somewhere in the nice, sweet woods and take a snooze, just like camping out. And then—in the morning, when the old sun comes sneaking up through the trees, we'll fool him! We won't wait till he can make it hot, but we'll get right up with the birds and the squirrels and we'll just run right along. And by twelve o'clock we'll be in Richmond—where they have good things to eat. So there you are—all mapped out. Only now we'll have a belt supper."

"A belt supper?" queried the child curiously, though her face brightened at the thought of *any* kind of supper, made out of belts or any other thing.

"Um-hum," asseverated her father gravely. "See— this is the way it's done."

He cupped his hands and took a draught from the spring, pretending to chew it as it went down. "You take a big drink of nice cold water; then draw up your belt as tight as you can—and say your prayers."

To his surprise his small daughter only sniffed scornfully.

"Oh, shucks, Daddy! I know a better way than that. Susan an' me used to do it all the time while you were away."

"What did you do?" he asked curiously, for he had forgotten that more than half the childish play world is the world of "make believe."

"Why, we—we just *'let on,'* " she answered, with simple naïveté. "Sit down an' I'll show you how."

He sat down obediently, but not before he had picked up an old tin can from nearby and set it carefully between them.

"This rock is our table—the moss is the table cloth. Oh, it isn't green," she cried as he looked down in serious doubt. "You must *help* me make believe. Now— doesn't it look nice and white?"

"It does, indeed. I can see nothing but snowy linen of the finest texture," he responded instantly.

"That's better," complimented his hostess. And then with a grand air—

"I'm so glad you dropped in, sir—an' just at supper time. Pass your plate an' allow me to help you to some batter bread."

"Batter bread! Ah, just what I was hoping for," her guest replied, thankfully extending his plate for the imaginary feast. "Thank you. Delicious. The very best I've tasted for a year. Did you make it yourself?"

"Oh, dear, no—the cook."

"Ah, of course! Pray pardon me. I might have known."

The little hostess inclined her head. "Take plenty of butter. 'Cause batter bread isn't good 'thout butter."

"Thank you—what lovely golden butter. And—goodness gracious! What is this I see before me? Can this really be a sausage?"

"Yes, sir," laughed Virgie with delight. "And there's the ham. I smoked it myself over hick'ry wood. Please help yourself."

She pretended to arrange a cup and saucer in front of her and held daintily in her fingers a pair of imaginary sugar tongs.

"Coffee? How many lumps? And *do* you take cream?"

"Five, please—and a little cream. There—just right."

She passed the cup gracefully and added a little moue of concern for the efficiency of her ménage.

"I'm afraid you won't find it very hot," said this surprising young hostess. "That butler of mine is growing absolutely *wuthless*."

"Then perhaps we can have something better," her guest responded readily, and he picked up the battered old tin can. "Permit me, Miss Cary, to offer you a glass of fine old blackberry wine which I carefully brought with me to your beautiful home. It has been in my family wine cellars since 1838.

"Well—" he cried, as Virgie suddenly sat back with a look of painful recollection on her face.

"Oh, Daddy," she murmured pathetically, "*don't* let's call it *blackberry* wine."

"Forgive me, darling," her father said tenderly, and he took the small face between his hands and kissed her. "There, now—it's all right. It's *all right*."

To create a diversion he looked behind him with a frown and spoke with great severity to an imaginary waiter.

"Here, *Jo*! How dare you bring such terribly reminiscent stuff to our table. Go get the port.

"We'll surely have to discharge that butler," he said. "He's too shiftless. And now, fair lady, will you honor me by joining the humblest of your admirers in a sip of port."

"With pleasure," answered his hostess, and lifted the can of water in both hands. "Your health, sir. May your shadow never grow littler."

Halfway through her drink Virgie stopped and slowly put the can down. She looked at her father, who already had his finger at his lips. Voices had come to them from down the road—the sounds of a party of men talking and laughing as they marched along.

Cary's face took on again the grim lines which had been wiped away momentarily by their little bit of play. He was trying to make himself believe that the approaching party might be friends, although he knew only too well that such a possibility was full of doubt. There were too many scouting parties of Federals ready to pounce on Rebel patrols in these perilous days to allow any but large forces of men to venture far from Richmond, and when his own men sallied forth they did not go with laughter but with tightly drawn, silent lips.

"S-s-s-h," he whispered, and held up his finger again, as she seemed ready to burst into questioning.

Immediately she snuggled close to him and whispered hotly in his ear, "Who are they, Daddy?"

"I don't know, honey," he whispered back. "But I'm afraid they're Yanks. Keep quiet till they pass." And quickly deserting the stone under the trees where they had had their "belt supper" he drew her with him behind the large ledge of rock from under which the spring flowed out. Looking behind them he saw that with good luck they could reach the shelter of the woods and get up over the hill without being seen. But just now they could not stir from their hiding place unless—unless the men were Confederates. This faint hope, however, soon flickered out when he saw the color of their uniforms.

Up the road came four dismounted men with a corporal in command. They were taking it easy as they walked along, their caps thrust back, their coats open and their Sharps' carbines carried in the variety of ways that a soldier adopts to ease his shoulder of the burden that grows heavier with every mile.

"Here's the place, boys," the Corporal called out as his eye fell on the spring. "We can get some decent water, now. That James River water's too yellow for any Northern man to put inside of him."

At the sound of a voice which he had heard that same morning while he hid in the attic of the overseer's cabin Cary's hold on his daughter's hand tightened warningly.

"Come along, Virgie," he whispered. "We'll get out of the way."

"But, Daddy," she protested in low tones, "we've got our pass."

"Yes, yes, I know," he answered, with a twinge of regret that the rest of the world could not trust so faithfully to human kindness. "But that's for emergency. Come along, honey—quick!"

Silently as a shadow the two stole out of the shelter of the ledge of rock, and by dint of keeping it between them and the troopers, managed to cover most of the open space between the spring and the protecting trees without being seen. Meanwhile, they heard the Corporal giving his commands.

"You, Collins, take sentry duty out there in the road for a while. As soon as we make the coffee we'll bring you out a cup. Now—over the wall with you, men."

Leaving one man behind to pace slowly up and down the dusty road the four sprang over the wall and advanced towards the spring. It was well the sight of the cool water held their eyes for if they had only looked up they might have seen Virgie wresting her hand out of her father's grasp and standing suddenly petrified with the thought that she had left behind her one beloved possession.

"Here's the spring, Smith—under the rock. Fill up the canteens. Here, Harry, help me get firewood."

With a soldier's readiness when it comes to making camp one of the troopers promptly collected the canteens and knelt down by the spring, carefully submerging one at a time so as to get the sweet, cold water in all its purity. Another opened the knapsacks and took out a can of coffee, biscuits and some scraps of meat—not much with which to make a meal but still so much more than many a Rebel soldier had that day as to take on the proportions of a feast. Meanwhile, Corporal Dudley had drawn his saber and was engaged in leisurely lopping off the dead branches of a fallen tree.

"This strikes me a lot better than the camp," he remarked as he tossed his firewood into a heap. "A man and his friends can have a quiet drink here, without treating a whole battalion."

His eye fell on the ground near the spring as he spoke and he paused. Then, with a grin on his face, he jabbed his saber into something which lay there and held it transfixed on the point.

"Say, boys—look at this," and he shook poor Susan Jemima till her arms and legs wiggled spasmodically

and her dress seemed on the point of complete disinte-
gration.

Perhaps, if Corporal Dudley had not laughed deri-
sively Virgie might have stayed hidden in the protection of the trees, but this outrageous insult combined
with the terrible sight of poor Susan Jemima impaled
on a Yankee sword was too much for her bursting heart.
With blazing eyes she broke away from her father and
dashed back to the group at the spring.

"Here, you! You stop that," she cried angrily at the
astonished troopers, who caught up their carbines at
the sound of feet. *"How dare you!"*

There was a moment of surprise and then the four
broke out in guffaws of laughter.

"Well, hang me if it isn't the little girl we saw this
morning," shouted Dudley, without, however, stopping
the torture of the defenseless Susan Jemima. "Where
did *you* drop from?"

"Ne'm min' where I dropped from," commanded the
wrathful Virgie with her dark eyes like twin stars of hate.
"You're the meanest old thing I ever saw. *Give me back
my baby!"*

Back in the trees a little way a man was watching
with a heavy heart. He knew only too well what was
to come. No matter what the final outcome might be
when he showed his safeguard to his own army's lines
there would be a delay and searching questions and

more of the old insults which always made his blood boil—which always made the increasing burden of despair still harder to bear. But there was no use in putting off the trial—Virgie had slipped away in spite of every whispered remonstrance and now that she was there in the center of that group of guffawing Yankees, there, too, was the only place for him. And so, he stepped out swiftly and faced the enemy.

"Hah!" shouted Dudley, looking up at the sound of branches crackling underfoot. "A Johnnie Reb, eh—walking right into camp! That's right, Harry, keep him covered."

He looked Cary over from head to foot with a sneer at his tattered uniform.

"Well, sir," he asked, "who are you?"

"A Confederate officer," was the quiet reply, "acting as escort for this child. We are on our way to Richmond."

Cary's hand went into the breast of his coat and he drew out a folded paper.

"Here is my authority for entering your lines—a pass signed by Lieutenant-Colonel Morrison."

At the sound of the name Corporal Dudley started and quickly took the paper. But before he opened it he gave Cary a keen look which, to the Confederate officer, did not bode well for the prospect of immediate release. It seemed as if the man's sharp wits had suddenly seized on something which he could profitably turn to his own account.

With his back turned on Cary and Virgie the Corporal unfolded the pass and studied it carefully, while the troopers gathered behind him and tried to read its contents over his shoulder.

"Pwhat does it say?" asked the young Irishman, Harry O'Connell, who had covered Cary with his carbine. " 'Tis a precious bit of paper, bedad—if it passes him through *me*."

"It says: 'Pass Virginia Cary and escort through all Federal lines, and assist them as far as possible in reaching Richmond,' " read the Corporal.

Deep in thought he turned the paper over and studied the name on the back. At the sight of the signature there his mouth fell open and he uttered a shout of surprise. His eyes brightened and he stepped back from the group and threw up his head with a look of triumph on his dark face. He struck the paper a slap with the back of his hand.

"Morrison on *one* side—and 'Old Bob' on the *other*," he exclaimed. "What luck! What a *find*."

"How so—a find?"

The man who had had to put his own brother under arrest a few short weeks before and then had seen him shot through the heart by this same officer whose name was on the pass looked at the questioner with an ugly glitter in his eyes. He was beginning to taste already the sweets of revenge. For blood ties bind, no matter how badly they are stretched, and long ago Corporal Dudley had sworn to wipe out his grudge.

"Why, man, can't you see?" he whispered excitedly. "This Johnnie Reb is the man that was hiding in the cabin loft this morning. Morrison lied when he said he wasn't there—you remember, he was the only one who looked—he lied and as soon as he got us out of the way he let him come down and he gave him *this*. Could any man ask for better proof that we had the spy right in our hands and then our commanding officer deliberately let him go?"

At the sound of the man's excited whispering Cary's fears as to the value of Virgie's pass grew too strong to warrant this agony of watching and waiting, and he stepped forward with a sharp question:

"Well, Corporal, isn't the pass satisfactory?"

"Oh, perfectly—perfectly," Dudley answered with baleful readiness, but made no move to return it.

Cary put out his hand. "Then I would like to have it again, if you please."

By way of answer Corporal Dudley carefully found an inside pocket and buttoned the pass up in his coat. "Oh, no, you don't," he said, with an evil grin. "I've got a better use for that little piece of paper."

"What do you mean?"

"I mean that you're my prisoner, Mister Johnnie Reb," was the brutal answer.

"For what?" asked Cary, while his heart grew sick inside him and his lips twitched. Richmond—and food for Virgie were growing farther away every moment.

"Because you're a Rebel *spy*, that's why," came the biting answer.

"Oh—none of that," as Cary's fists doubled up and he made a forward step at the Corporal. "I guess you know what's good for you, with three guns at your back. If Colonel Morrison wouldn't take you as a spy, *I will!*"

"Here, boys," he said in brusque command to his men, "we'll have to cut the supper and take this man to camp. There'll be a sunrise hanging tomorrow or I miss my guess. Come on, now. Bring him along."

"Wait a minute, Corporal," O'Connell said. "Sure I've something to say to ye," and he led him aside where the others could not hear.

All unconscious of the fatal predicament into which Susan Jemima and she had got them Virgie looked up at her father from where she stood in the shelter of his arm.

"Daddy," she questioned, in a small, puzzled voice, "what are they going to do?"

"S-s-s-h," her father commanded as he patted her head comfortingly. "Everything will be all right, honey, I'm sure." But he had caught enough of the Corporal's altercation with Trooper O'Connell to make him see that things were very far from being what he wanted Virgie to suppose.

"Ye'd better be careful now," O'Connell said to Dudley. "Ye know well that if the pass is all right ye'll be getting yerself into a peck o' trouble."

"It isn't *me* that'll get in trouble," Dudley answered, with grim triumph. "It's someone else."

"Faith, then, *who?*" was the query.

"Morrison," snapped Dudley, with an ominous click of his teeth.

"The Colonel? Why?"

"*Because he helped this spy escape!* That's why. He killed my brother, shot him. Shot him down like a dog. But now I'm even with him."

He shook the pass under the trooper's nose and crowed with satisfaction.

"I've been waiting for a chance like this," he chortled, "and now I'm going to make him sweat—sweat blood."

"Don't be a fool, Corporal," the trooper counseled. "What'll ye be after doin'?"

"*Report him at headquarters*—for helping a spy escape! If I have the man and *this*," and he slapped the paper, "it'll mean his sword and shoulder straps—if not a bullet! Come on!"

He turned away, to scramble over the wall, but Trooper O'Connell caught his arm.

"Hold on! Ye may get in trouble."

In answer Dudley broke away and doggedly kept on towards the stone wall and the road. "Keep off," he snarled. "*I'm* running this."

"I know ye are," the trooper replied, "but wait," and he pointed to the rear. "Don't forget that the Colonel's out yonder reconnoiterin'. If he happened to overtake ye on the road—"

Struck with the sudden thought Dudley paused. "Well, that's so," he growled as he saw how easily he could be held for disobeying orders and how quickly all his plans for vengeance could be smashed. He stood still for a moment gnawing his lip, then suddenly struck his doubled fist into the palm of the other hand.

"Then you stay here to guard the prisoner," he said. "I'll cut through the woods—make my report—come back with the horses—and my authority."

"Here, Smith! You and Judson come along with me. Never mind the grub. We'll get that later."

Turning to O'Connell, "If you hear anyone coming, take those two into the woods. Collins! You'll have to stay on sentry duty till I get back. If any troops pass here, get out of sight at once and give Harry warning. Now, boys—come along with me—we'll take it on the trot," and climbing quickly over the wall the man who held two lives in the hollow of his hand ran down the road with the two troopers, finally cutting over into the woods and disappearing from view.

Cary and Virgie stood still by the spring. Out in the

road the sentry paced back and forth. Behind them Trooper O'Connell stood on guard, his carbine in his arms across his breast.

Virgie pulled gently at her father's hand.

"Daddy," she whispered, "are they—are they goin' to carry us off to the Yankee camp?"

"I'm afraid so, darling, but I don't know," he answered sadly. "We'll just have to wait. Wait," he repeated, as he sat down on a rock and drew her close to him. Without being seen either by Virgie or O'Connell he picked up a jagged stone the size of his fist and hid it under his knee against the rock. It would be a poor weapon at best, but Cary had grown desperate and if the trooper once turned his back and gave him opportunity poor Harry O'Connell would wake up with a very bad headache and Virgie would be in Richmond.

But Virgie's eyes were on neither the hidden stone nor her father's watchful, relentless face. All that Virgie could see was a knapsack open on the ground and food—real food displayed round about with a prodigality which made her mouth water and her eyes as big as saucers.

"Daddy," she murmured, clutching at his sleeve, "while we are waitin' do you reckon we could take just a *little* bit of that?"

"No, dear—not now," her father answered, with a touch of impatience. It would be too much, even in those bitter times, to accept a man's food and then break his head for it.

"Well," said Virgie, completely mystified at the restraint, "I don't see why they shouldn't be polite to us. We were just as polite as could be when the Yankees took our corn."

Just then the young Irishman with the carbine turned around and caught the wan look on Virgie's face and the hunger appeal in her big dark eyes. At once a broad smile broke over his freckled countenance and he gestured hospitably with his gun.

"Have somethin' to eat, little wan."

Cary's knee loosened. The jagged stone fell to the ground.

"Thank you, old fellow," he cried, springing to his feet. "I can't show my gratitude to you in any substantial way at present—but God bless you, just the same." He dropped down on the rock again and hid his face in his hands. Another moment and the kindhearted trooper might have been lying face downwards in the muddy ground around the spring. It had been only touch-and-go, but the man's warm Irish heart had saved him.

"Oh, that's all right, sir," O'Connell answered freely. "Sure an' I'd like to see ye get through, though I ain't the Gineral. At least, not yet," he grinned.

"There ye are, little girl," he went on, pushing the knapsack over towards Virgie with the muzzle of his

carbine. "Jist help yerself—an' give yer dad some, too."

With a little cry of delight Virgie swooped down on the knapsack and explored its interior with eager hands.

"I'm much obliged, Mr. Yankee. We cert'n'y do need it—bad." She tossed the tangled hair back from her eyes and looked thankfully up at this curious person who had so much food that he could really give part of it away. "Please, Mr. Yankee—won't you tell me your name?"

"Harry O'Connell, at your service, miss."

"Thank you," she bowed. "I'm very glad to meet you." Then her searching hands found something wonderful in the knapsack and she sprang up and ran with her prizes to her father.

"Look, Daddy—*two biscuits!* Take one. It's—it's *real!*"

Cary's eyes grew moist.

"Thank you, darling. Thank you." Just now the lump in his throat would not have allowed him to eat soup, let alone a rather hard biscuit, but he looked up with a laugh and waved a genial salute to the trooper, who as genially responded.

Virgie, however, had become quite single minded since she had discovered food, and with a happy sigh she raised the biscuit to her lips. Just then the sentry in the road flung up his hand with a shout.

"Look out, O'Connell! They're coming," and he

clambered quickly over the wall and dropped behind it, his gun in readiness.

"What is it?" demanded the other trooper.

"Detachment of cavalry. A small one."

"But whose is it, man. Can ye not see?"

Collins, holding his hand behind him in a gesture which commanded them to stay where they were, raised his head cautiously over the wall.

"Morrison's," he answered, after a quick look, and he dropped down again out of sight.

At the sound of hoof beats and the name she remembered so well Virgie, with her biscuit all untasted, sprang up from the ground as if she would run out on the road. But her father caught her, for O'Connell had turned to them with a serious face.

"I'm sorry, sir, but I'll have to trouble ye to get under cover in the woods. No argymint, sir," he said decisively, as he saw some show of resistance on Cary's part. "I'm under orders."

"Yes, yes, I know," Cary cried, impatiently, "but I want to speak to Colonel Morrison. I *must* speak to him. Give me a moment, man. You won't ever regret it."

"Come now—none o' that," commanded the trooper, pushing him back with the carbine across his breast. "Don't make me use force, sir. Ye'll have to go—so go quietly. And mind—no shenanigan!"

Cary stood his ground for a moment, meeting the

trooper eye to eye—then turned with hanging head and walked a few steps back into the woods.

"Come, Virgie," he said, "I guess we won't get to see Colonel Morrison after all."

But Virgie, being a woman, had her own ideas about what she would or would not do. At the same moment that the trooper was forcing her father step by step back into the woods, Virgie was running madly towards the stone wall and before either of the soldiers could stop her she had clambered up on its broad top and was calling out to a man who clattered by at the head of a troop of cavalry.

"Colonel Morrison! Colonel Morrison!"

Chapter Eight

H alt!"

At the sound of that piping, childish treble calling his name in so unexpected a place the officer at the head of the troop threw up his gauntleted hand and brought the detachment to a standstill in a cloud of dust.

"Hello, there," he said, turning curiously around in his saddle. "Who is it wants me?"

"It's *me*, Virgie!" the child cried, leaping up and down on the wall, all forgetful of her sore foot. "Come help Daddy and me—come quick!"

"Well—what on earth—"

Morrison threw out a command to his men and, wheeling his horse, spurred vigorously up to the wall where he dismounted and came up to take a closer view of the tangle haired little person dancing on one foot.

"Why—bless my soul if it isn't Virgie!" His arms opened to take her in when, suddenly, his eye fell on

O'Connell, standing at attention on the other side of the wall.

"O'Connell," he said, sternly, "what is the meaning of this? Why aren't you with your detachment?"

"It isn't *his* fault," Virgie interposed in stout defense of the nice Yankee who carried biscuits in his knapsack. "He's under orders."

The glib use of the military term made a smile flicker across Morrison's face, but his eyes did not leave the troubled trooper.

"*Whose* orders?" he demanded.

"Corporal Dudley, sir," was the stammering answer.

At this moment Cary stepped forward and the two officers exchanged nods of recognition.

"Let me explain," the Confederate said. "Virgie and I were making for Richmond as rapidly as we could. Here, by this spring, we were put under arrest by a corporal and four troopers. Naturally, I presented your pass, but the corporal refused to honor it. He then left me under guard and hurried off to headquarters with the pass in his possession."

At this unwelcome news Morrison's head jerked back as if he had been struck and his lips tightened. Without the addition of another word to Cary's story he saw all the dire consequences to himself of what had been an act of the commonest humanity. Yes, in other times it would have been what any right thinking human being would have done for another in distress, but, unhappily, this was war time and the best of motives were only too often misread. In his mind's eye he saw the vindictive Dudley, eager for a revenge which he could not encompass any other way, laying the proof of this act before his superiors with an abundance of collateral evidence which, he knew, would condemn him before any military tribunal in the world. It mattered not what kindly impulses had guided his hand when he wrote the safeguard on the other side of the paper on which Robert E. Lee had previously placed his name, for it is not the custom of courts martial to weigh the milk of human kindness against the blood and iron of war. The good and the safety of the greater number demand the sacrifice of every man who would imperil the cause by ill considered generosity. Morrison could see that very presently he would have to answer certain stern questions.

Yet, there was a chance still that Dudley might be headed off and this whole miserable business stopped before revenge could set the inexorable wheels in motion and he whirled round on O'Connell with a sharp question:

"Which way did Dudley go?"

"Down the pike, then over the hill by the wood road, sir—makin' for headquarters," the young Irishman answered, only too glad of a chance to help his officer out of what, he saw, was a frightful situation.

"How long ago?" came back the instant query.

"Five minutes, sir. Ye cud catch him wid a horse."

"Ah," exclaimed Morrison, and he threw up his hand to his men. "Lieutenant Harris," he shouted. "Take a squad and ride to camp by the wood road. Overtake Corporal Dudley or intercept him at headquarters. Don't fail! Get him and bring him here!"

Lieutenant Harris's hand went up to his hat in ready salute and he bellowed out his orders.

"Jennings! Hewlett! Brown! Hammond! Burt! 'Bout face. Forward!" Almost before the words were out of his mouth Harris and his men were riding madly down the road in a chase, which the Lieutenant suspected, meant something more to his colonel, than merely the recovery of a safe-conduct for a Confederate officer and a little girl.

Morrison turned to Trooper O'Connell and jerked his thumb towards the road.

"Report at my quarters this evening—at nine," he said curtly. And the young Irishman, thankful to be well out of the mess, quickly clambered over the wall and disappeared though not without a soft voiced fare-well from Virgie.

"Good-by, Mr. Knapsack Man," called the child. "Thank you for the biscuits."

Then Cary came forward and gripped the other's hand.

"Colonel," he said earnestly, with full appreciation of what was passing through Morrison's mind, "I hope no trouble will come of this. If I had only known the vindictiveness of this man—"

He was interrupted by a genially objecting hand and a laugh which Morrison was somehow able to make lighthearted.

"Oh, that will be all right. Harris will get him—never fear."

"And so," he said, addressing Miss Virginia, "that bad man took your pass?"

"Yes, sir. He did," Virgie answered, and caught his hand in hers. "He ran right away with it—mean old thing."

"Well, then—we'll have to write you out another one. A nice, clean, white one this time. Come on, little sweetheart. We'll do it together," and he took out a note book and pencil.

"I say, Morrison," Cary murmured, glancing apprehensively at the troopers idling in the road and very plainly interested in what the small group were doing, "do you really think you'd better—on your own account?"

Again Morrison's hand was raised in polite objection. He had taken a sporting chance when he wrote the pass which had been stolen but because he had probably lost was no reason why he shouldn't play the game out bravely to the end. So he only smiled at Virgie, who came and sat beside him, and began to write the few short sentences of his second safe-conduct. But while he wrote he was talking in low tones which the troopers in the road could not hear.

"There's a line of your pickets about three miles up the road, Cary," said he. "If I loaned you a horse, do you think Virgie could ride behind you?"

"*Me?*" pouted Virgie. "Why, Daddy says that when I was bornded, I came ridin' in on a stork."

Morrison burst out laughing and dropped his hand down on the small paw resting on his knee.

"Then, by St. George and the Dragon we'll send you home to Jefferson Davis on a snorting Pegasus!"

Again Cary spoke to him in warning tones, which at the same time thanked him unendingly for the kindly thought.

"You needn't trouble about the mount. Why, man," he said huskily, "you're in trouble enough, as it is! And if our lines are as close as you say they are—"

Once more the Union officer checked him.

"It isn't any trouble. Only—you'll have to be careful of your approach, even to your own lines. Those gray devils in the rifle pits up there have formed the habit of shooting *first* and asking questions *afterwards*. There you are," and he tore the leaf from his note book and handed it up with a faint smile.

The Southerner took it with a reluctant hand.

"I—I wish I could thank you—Morrison," he said in tones that shook with feeling, "but you see I—I—"

"Then please don't try. Because if you do I'll—I'll have to hold Virgie as a prisoner of war."

"Well, young one," he said to the small Miss Cary with a laugh, "did you really get something to eat?"

"Yes, sir. That is—we *almost* did."

"*Almost?*" he echoed.

"Yes, sir," came the plaintive answer. "Eve'y time we start to eat—somethin' *always* happens!"

"Well, well, that *is* hard luck," he said with a gentle squeeze of her frail body. "But I'll bet you it won't happen this time; not if a whole regiment tries to stop it."

"Come on," he suggested as he sprang to his feet and began picking up dry twigs. "You can start in and munch on those heavenly biscuits while this terrible Yankee builds the fire." Cary made a move as if to help; but Morrison checked him.

"Oh, no, Cary, just you keep on sitting still. This is no work for you. You're tired out.

"Here, Virgie, I know you want to get me some water from the spring. Please pick out some of the cleanest water you can and put it carefully in the coffee pot. All right. There you are. *'Tention!* Carr-ee coffee pot! Right wheel! *March!*"

With a carefree laugh he turned away to light the little heap of twigs he had placed between two flat stones. "It's mighty considerate of my boys to leave us all these things. We'll call it the raid of Black Gum Spring.

"And here comes the little lady with the coffee pot filled just right. Now watch me pour in the good old coffee—*real* coffee, Virgie dear—not made from aco'ns." He settled the pot on the fire and sat back with a grin. "Oh, oh! Don't watch it," he cried, in well feigned alarm as Virgie, unwilling to believe the sight, stooped over to feast her eyes on the rich brown powder sinking into the black gulf of the pot. "If you do that it will never, *never* boil!"

"All right," the child agreed pathetically, and she sank wearily down against her father's knee. "I'll just pray for it to hurry up."

The two men exchanged quiet smiles and Cary murmured something in his daughter's ear.

"Oh, no, I won't," she answered, and then looked up at Morrison with a roguish light in her dark eyes. "He's only afraid I'll pray so terribly hard that the old coffee pot will boil over an' put out the fire."

Morrison, chuckling, now began to drag something out of a rear pocket. Presently, he uncorked it and held it up—a *flask!*

"Here, Cary," he said, holding out a cup. "Join me, won't you? Of course, you understand—in case a snake should bite us."

"Colonel Morrison," responded the Southerner, "you are certainly a man of ideas."

He waited for his foe to fill his own cup, then raised his in a toast:

"I drink to the health, sir, of you and yours. Here's hoping that some day I may take *you* prisoner!"

At the quizzical look of surprise in the other's face Cary's voice almost broke.

"I mean, sir, it's the only way I could ever hope to show you how much I appreciate—"

He stopped and covered his face with his hands, not a little to his daughter's alarm.

"Come, come, old chap," the Northerner said bluffly, tapping him on the shoulder. "Brace up. It's the fortunes of war, you know. One side or the other is bound to win. Perhaps—who knows—it may be *your* turn to-morrow. Well, sir—here goes. May it soon be over—in the way that's best and wisest for us all.

"Now, Virgie," he went on, when the toast had been drunk, "while I wash these cups suppose you go on another voyage of discovery through the magic knapsack for some sugar for the coffee."

He watched her fling herself impetuously on the knapsack. "If you find any Yankee spoons—put them under arrest. They haven't any pass like yours."

Then he turned to Cary: "Have any trouble on the road as you came along?"

The other man shook his head.

"None to speak of. We were stopped several times of course, but each time your pass let us through without delay—until we met Dudley. And now I'm worried, Colonel," he said frankly, while his eyes tried to tell the other all that he feared without putting it in words, "worried on your account. It's easy to see that the man has a grudge against you—"

"Yes, I'm afraid he has," was the thoughtful reply. "But really, Cary, you mustn't try to carry any more burdens than your own, just now. I know what you mean and what, I daresay, you'd be only too willing to do, but I can't permit it."

They were interrupted by the spectacle of Virgie standing before them with anxiously furrowed brow, a paper bag in one hand and three spoons clutched in the other.

"But Colonel Morrison," she was saying in tragic tones, "there isn't a drop of milk."

"Milk!" he cried in mock despair. "Well, dash my buttons if I didn't forget to order a cow."

"Oh, *I* know what to do," cried the child. Dropping her supplies and utensils she ran to the wall and climbed up.

"Hey, there, *you*," commanded the small general with an imperious gesture to the assembled troopers. "One of you men ride right over to camp and bring us back some milk—an' butter."

At this abrupt demand of so small a rebel on the commissary of the United States a roar of laughter went up from the troopers, though some of them had the grace to salute and so relieve the child of embarrassment.

"Virgie! Virgie!" called her father, scandalized.

"It's all right, Cary," Morrison laughed. "She's only starting in at giving orders a little earlier than most women.

"Never you mind, Miss Brigadier," he comforted. "We'll have all those luxuries next time, or when I come to see you in Richmond after the war is over. Just now we'll do the best we can. Come along."

Virgie got down from the wall and pattered up to the fire.

"Is it ready yet?" she asked with the perfect directness of seven years.

"In a minute now. Ah-hah! There she goes."

He took the pot from the fire and set it down on a rock where, presently, he brought a cupful of cold water to pour in.

"Is that to settle it?" she asked of her father.

"Yes, child—and I wish all our questions were as easily cleared up. And now—to the attack."

"Right-o. Virgie—pass the beautiful, hand painted china and let's fill up. This one for your daddy—you can put the sugar in. Only don't burn those precious fingers."

Virgie carried the steaming cup to her father and put it in his hands with shining eyes.

"This is better than our old belt supper, Daddy, isn't it?" she said, with a flirt of her tangled curls. "Anyway —it *smells* nicer."

She was back at the sugar bag at once, digging out spoonfuls for Morrison's coffee.

"Thank you, Miss Cary, I am indeed obliged to you. Now do sit down and *eat*. No, not another word till you've eaten two whole biscuits!"

For several ecstatic moments the child munched her biscuits. It had been a long time since she had eaten anything so delicious, although if those same biscuits had appeared on the Cary table a month ago they would have probably been scorned. But eager as her appetite was it did not stop the active workings of her mind and she presently was struck by an idea which tried to force itself out through a mouthful of biscuit—with the usual amusing results.

"*Virginia!*" admonished her father.

Morrison laughed out like a boy and slapped his knee.

"Suppose we swallow—and try again."

Virgie, thus adjured, concentrated her mind on the task—gulped, blinked, swallowed with pathetically straining eyes, and then smiled triumphantly.

"Excuse me, Daddy. I guess I wasn't very polite."

"Apology accepted. What were you going to say?"

The child looked up with a sweetly serious look in her eyes that the two men recognized as the forerunner of true womanly thought for others.

"I was only goin' to ask the Colonel if he didn't think his men out there would like some of these *heavingly*

things to eat?" she said plaintively. "It must be terrible
—jus' to look on!"

"Well, bless your little heart," the Northerner cried.
"But don't you worry about the boys. They'll have theirs
when they get back to camp. Go on and eat, Virgie.
Stuff in another biscuit. And, look! By Jupiter, *butter*!"

Evidently Trooper O'Connell during the past twenty-
four hours had foraged or blarneyed most successfully
for out of the knapsack which he had left behind Morrison suddenly produced a small earthenware jam jar
in which was something now indubitably liquid in form
but none the less sweet, yellow, appetizing butter. Pouring a little on a biscuit he held it out to her, speculating
on what she would say.

The tot took it hungrily and raised it to her lips, her
eyes shining and her face glowing with anticipation.
Then she paused and, with a little cry of vexation over
her selfishness, held out the biscuit to her father.

"Here, Daddy," she said. "You take this—because
you tried to bring me somethin' good to eat yesterday."

The father threw a look at Morrison and caught Virgie to him in a swift embrace.

"No, dear," he said. "Eat your nice buttered biscuit
and thank the good Lord for it. Your father will get
more fun out of seeing you eat that little bit than he
would out of owning a whole cellar of big stone crocks
jam full. Do you know—I think when we get up to Rich-

mond you'll have to write a letter to the Colonel—a nice long letter, thanking him for all he's done. Won't you?"

There was a pause for a moment as the child looked over at Morrison, revolving the thought in her mind.

The Union officer had passed into a sudden reverie, the hand holding his coffee cup hanging listlessly over his knee. He was thinking of another little girl, and one as dear to him as this man's child was to her father. He was wondering if the fortunes of war would ever let him see her face again or hear her voice—or feel her chubby arms around his neck. She was very, very far away—well cared for, it was true, but he knew only too well that it would need but one malignant leaden missile to make her future life as full of hardships as those which the little tot beside him was passing through today. So much, at least, for the ordinary chances of war—he was beginning to wonder how much had been added to these perils by the matter of the pass and whether his superiors would see the situation as it had appeared to his eyes.

Into this sad reverie Virgie's soft voice entered with a gentleness which roused but did not startle him. When she spoke, it seemed as if some subtle thought-current between their minds had put the subject of his dreams into the child's mind.

"Do you reckon," the child said, curiously, "that Gertrude is havin' *her* supper now?"

The Union officer looked up with eyes that mutely blessed her.

"Yes, dear, I was thinking of her—and her mother."

Again he was silent for a space, and when he spoke, his voice was dreamy, tender, as he seemed to look with unseeing eyes far into the Northland where dwelt the people of his heart.

"Do you know, Cary, this war for us, the men, may be a hell, but what is it for those we leave at home? The women! Who wait—and watch—and too often watch in vain. *We* have the excitement of it—the rush—the battles—and we think that ours is the harder part when, in reality, we make our loved ones' lives a deeper, blacker hell than our own. Theirs to watch and listen with the love hunger in their hearts, month in, month out and often without a word! Theirs to starve on the crusts of hope! Waiting—always waiting! Hunting the papers for the thing they dread to find; a name among the missing. A name among the dead! Good Heaven! When I think of it sometimes—" Morrison dropped his head between his clenched fists and groaned.

"Yes, yes, old fellow, I know," the other man answered, for in truth he *did* know, "but I want you to remember that for you the crusts of hope will some day be the bread of life—and love."

Slowly the Northerner's face came up out of his hands

and he seemed to take heart again. After all, he had led a charmed life so far—perhaps the God of Battles had written his name among those who would some day go back to live the life for which the Almighty made them. God grant then that he might have for his friend this man who, in the time of his own greater grief, was unselfish enough to console him. Ah! If God would only grant that from this day on there would be no more of this hideous fighting. Morrison's eyes met the other's and he put out his hand.

Suddenly there came the sound of a shot. Another and another—then a volley, which almost at once became a continuous rattle of musketry.

The Northerner sprang to his feet. "Look! There go your pickets."

Struck dumb by this sudden return to the actualities of life the two men stood motionless, listening for every sound which might tell them what it meant. For a little while they had dreamed the dream of peace only to have it rudely shattered.

But Virgie had not followed them in their dreams, for she was an extremely practical young lady. Having seen food, real food, vanish away before her very eyes several times already she was quite prepared to see it happen again.

"There!" she said, in tones in which prophecy and resignation were oddly mingled. "Didn't I jus' *know* somethin' was goin' to happen!"

By this time Morrison had run to the stone wall and sprung to its top. Out in the road the troopers had mounted without waiting for command and with one accord had faced towards the firing.

"Can you see anything?" Cary called.

"Not yet," said Morrison. "I guess we came too close to your nest—and the hornets are coming out."

"Turner!" he commanded, and a trooper's hand went up, "ride up to the fork of the road. Learn what you can and report."

As the cavalryman struck his heels into his horse's sides and dashed up the road Cary put the wishes of both men into words.

"It's too near sundown for a battle. It will only be a skirmish."

"Ye-e-e-s, possibly," the Northerner assented, and he looked thoughtfully at Virgie, "but still—"

"What is it?"

"I can't send you forward now—in the face of that fire. And, for that matter, I can't send you to the rear. In five minutes this road will be glutted with cavalry and guns."

"Never mind, Morrison," the Southerner returned. "I couldn't go now—anyway."

"Why?"

Cary opened out his hands in a simple gesture. "Because, in case of trouble for you at headquarters, I'm *still* your prisoner." With his eyes brave and steady on

the others he took the newly written pass from his breast
—and tore it in pieces. "When you want me," he said,
"you'll find me—*here*."

If there had been time for argument Morrison would
have hotly protested against such self-sacrifice, but
events were crowding upon them too fast. From down
the road came the sound of furious galloping. Almost
at once Lieutenant Harris, riding hard at the head of a
troop of cavalry, swept round the curve and drew his
horse upon his haunches.

"Colonel Morrison!" he shouted. "You are ordered—"

"One moment, Lieutenant," interrupted Morrison in
tones so even that Cary marveled at his composure, "*Did
you get Corporal Dudley?*"

Cary's ears ached for the answer. He knew just as
well as the questioner the danger which might now be
disclosed or be forever forgotten and his heart went out
to the other in this moment of hideous suspense.

There was an instant of hesitation and then came the
answer.

"*No, sir!* We tried hard but couldn't make it."

Morrison's face did not change but his hands tightened until the nails dug deep into his palms. He had
played—and lost.

"Go on with your report," he said.

Harris pulled in his fretting horse and delivered his
significant news.

"The Rebels are advancing in force. I was sent back to you with orders to join Major Foster at the fork and hold the road at any cost. Two light field pieces are coming to your support. Our main batteries are back there—in the woods."

"Right," said Morrison, "we go at once." Turning back to Virgie he caught her up in his arms and kissed her. "Good-by, little sweetheart. Hide under the rocks and keep close."

"Good-by, Morrison," Cary said, as they struck hands. "I can't wish you luck—but our hearts are with you as a man."

"Thanks, old fellow," said the enemy, as he sprang over the wall. "It helps—God knows."

He caught at his horse's mane and threw himself into the saddle without touching the stirrup, while his voice roared out his command.

"Ready, men! Forward!"

"Good-by," shrilled Virgie in her childish treble. "Good-by, Colonel! Don't get hurt."

"Daddy!" she cried, as they crouched down in their hiding place behind the wall. "Is there going to be a— a *battle*?"

"Only a little one. But you won't be afraid."

A rattle of approaching wheels came from down the road, the shock of steel tires striking viciously against the stones, the cries and oaths of the drivers urging the horses forward.

"Look!" cried Cary, springing to his feet in spite of the danger in which his gray uniform placed him. "Here come the field pieces. In a minute now the dogs will begin to bark."

With a roar of wheels and a clash of harness and accouterments the guns rushed by while the child stared and stared, her big eyes almost starting out of her face.

"The dogs!" she said in wonder. "There wasn't a single dog there!"

"Another kind of dog," her father said with a meaning look. "And their teeth are *very* long. Ah! There they go! Over yonder on the hill—in the edge of the woods. The Yankee dogs are barking. Now listen for the answer."

Together they listened, father and daughter, with straining ears—listened for the defiant reply of those men who, being Americans, were never beaten until hunger and superior numbers forced them to the wall.

"Boom!" A great, ear-filling sound crashed over the hills and rolled, echoing, through the woods.

"That's us! That's us!" the man cried out exultantly, while he caught the child closer in his arms. "Hear our people talking, honey? Hear 'em talk!"

But overhead something was coming through the air and the child shrank down in terror—something that whined and screamed as it sped on its dreadful way and seemed like a demon out of hell searching for his prey.

"Lord a' mercy, Daddy!" the child cried out. "What's *that*?"

He patted her head consolingly. "Nothing at all but a shell. They sound much worse than they really are. Don't be afraid. Nothing will hurt you."

From the forks of the road the sound of volley firing grew stronger and, as if in response, the road to the Union rear now turned into a stream of living blue, with cavalry madly galloping and sweating infantry hurrying forward as fast as their legs could carry them.

"Look, Virgie, look!" her father cried, holding her head a little way above the wall. "See those bayonets shining back there across the road. A whole regiment of infantry. And they're going up against our men across an *open field*! By Jiminy, but those Yanks will get a mustard bath. Ah-hah!" he chortled, as a roar of musketry broke out. "I told you so! Our boys are after them. Good work! Good work!"

But again a shell passed over them and again the world was filled with that awful whining, shrieking sound.

"Daddy," the child cried, with quivering lips, but still dry eyed. "I don't *like* those things. I don't *like* 'em."

"There, there, darling," he comforted as they shrank closer under the protection of the wall. "Keep down under my arm and they won't bother you."

As he spoke a twig with a fresh yellow break in it fell

from a tree and struck his upturned face. He winced at the thought that the bullet might have flown a few feet lower. And meanwhile the sound of the firing came steadily closer.

"By Jove!" he murmured to himself, "it's a bigger rumpus than I thought."

This indeed was true. What had at first promised to be only a skirmish between the outposts of the two entrenched armies, now developed into a general engagement covering a space of half a mile along the line. A reconnoitering force of Federal cavalry had ridden too close to the rifle pits of the Confederates, and, as Morrison himself expressed it, "the hornets came out and began to sting."

Major Foster, commanding a larger force of cavalry, rode out in support of his reconnoitering party, and found himself opposed, not by a straggling line of Rebel pickets, but by a moving wall of tattered gray, the units of which advanced on a low-bent run, crouching behind some bush or stone, to fire, reload and advance again.

An aide raced back to the Union lines to ask for help in support of Foster's slender force of cavalry; and thus the order came to Morrison to join the detachment and hold the enemy until reënforcements could be formed and pushed to the firing line.

The delay, however, was well nigh fatal for Morrison and Major Foster, and from the point where Cary and little Virgie watched, the case of the Union horsemen seemed an evil one. True, that infantry and guns were soon advancing to their aid on a "double-quick"; yet all the advantage seemed to lie with the ragged, sharp-shooting Southerners.

The crackle of musketry increased; the dust rolled up and intermingled with the wreathes of drifting smoke, and through it came the vicious whine of leaden messengers of death.

Then, borne on the wind, came a sound that he would know till his dying day—*the rebel yell*. An exultant scream,—a cry of unending hate, defiance, *victory*!

He sprang to his feet. Off came the battered old campaign hat and unmindful that he stood there hidden in the woods and that his voice could carry only a few yards against the roar of battle, he swung it over his head and shouted out his encouragement.

"Look! We're whipping 'em. Virgie, do you hear? We're getting them on the run. Come on, boys! Come on!"

He felt her clutch on his sleeve. With wide eyes grown darker than ever with excitement, she asked her piteous question.

"Daddy! *Will they kill the Colonel?*"

For a moment he could not answer. Then, with a groan he gave back his answer: "I *hope* not, darling. I hope not!"

Down the road a riderless horse was coming, head up and stirrups flying. As it galloped past Cary scrutinized it closely and was glad he did not recognize it. In its wake came soldiers, infantry and dismounted cavalry, firing, retreating, loading and firing again, but always retreating.

"Here come the stragglers," he cried. "We're whipping 'em! Close, darling, *close*. Lie down against the wall."

He crouched above her, shielding her as best he could with his body. Then, suddenly, a man in blue leaped on the wall not ten feet away. He had meant to seize the wall as a breastwork and fight from behind it, but before he dropped down he would fire one last shot. His gun came up to his shoulder—he aimed at some unseen foe and fired. But from somewhere, out of the crash of sound and the rolling powder smoke, a singing missile came and found its mark. The man in blue bent over suddenly, wavered, then toppled down inside the wall, his gun ringing on the stones as he fell.

"Daddy!" the child whispered, with ashen face, "it's the biscuit man. It's HARRY!"

Her father's hand went out instinctively to cover her eyes. "Don't look, dear! Don't look!"

The road was choked now. Cavalry and infantry, all in a mad rush for the rear, were tearing by while the two field pieces which but a moment ago had gone into action with such a deadly whirl came limping back with slashed traces and splintered wheels. With fascinated eyes the Rebel officer watched from behind his wall, while everything, even his child, was forgotten in the lust for victory. And so he did not hear the faint voice behind him that cried out in an agony of thirst and pain.

"Water! Water! Help! Someone—give water!"

Virgie, with dilated eyes and heaving breast, crouched low as long as she could and then gave up everything to the pitiful appeal ringing in her ears. Quick as a flash, she sped away on bare feet over rocks and sharp, pointed branches of fallen trees to the spring, where she caught up a cup and filled it to the brim. Another swift rush and she reached the fallen man in blue and had the cup at his lips, while her arm went under his head to lift it.

"Virgie!" her father cried, frantic at the sight. With a great leap he was at her side, forcing her down to the ground and covering her with his body.

The trooper's head sank back and his eyes began to dull.

"May God bless ye, little one," he murmured. "Heaven—*Mary*—!" His lips give out one long, shuddering sigh. His body grew slack and his chin fell. Trooper Harry O'Connell had fought his last fight—had passed to his final review.

One look at the boyish face so suddenly gone gray and bloodless and Cary caught Virgie up in his arms. "Come, dear, you can't help him any more," and with a crouching run they were back once more in the shelter of the wall.

And now the shriek of the shells and the whine of the bullets came shriller than before. All around them the twigs were dropping, while the acrid powder smoke rolled in through the trees and burnt their eyes and throats. Again came men in blue retreating and among them an officer on horseback, wheeling his animal madly around among them and shouting encouragement as he tried to face them to the front. "Keep at it, men," Morrison was crying, half mad with rage. "One decent stand and we can hold them. Give it to them hard. Stand, I tell you. *Stand!*"

All around him, however, men were falling and those who were left began to waver. "Steady, men! Don't flinch," came the shout again. "Ah-hah, you *would*, would you? *Coward!*"

Morrison's sword held flatwise, thudded down on the back of a man who had flung away his gun. "Get back in the fight, you dog! Get back!"

He whipped out his revolver and pointed it till the gun had been snatched up, then fired all its chambers at the oncoming hordes in gray.

"One more stand," he yelled. "One more—"

Beside him the color sergeant gave a moan and bent in the middle like a hinge. Another slackening of his body and the stricken bearer of the flag plunged from his saddle, the colors trailing in the dust.

Morrison spurred his mount toward the fallen man, bending to grasp the colors from the tight gripped hand;

but even as he bent, his horse went down. He leaped to save himself, then turned once more, snatched at the flag of his routed regiment and waved it above his head.

"*Stand, boys, and give it to 'em!*"

A shout went up—not from the men he sought to rally to his flag, but from those who would win it at a cost of blood, for his troopers were running on a backward road, and Morrison fought alone. The "gray devils" were all around him now, and he backed against the wall, fighting till his sword was sent spinning from his fist by the blow of a musket butt; then, grasping the color-pole in both his hands, he parried bayonet thrusts and saber strokes, panting, breathing in hot, labored gasps, and cursing his enemies from a hoarse, parched throat.

A hideous, unequal fight it was, and soon Lieutenant-Colonel Morrison must fall as his colors fell and be trampled in the dust; yet now through an eddying drift of smoke came another ragged Southerner, a grim, gaunt man whose voice was as hoarse as Morrison's, who had grasped a saber from the blood-stained rocks and waved it above his head.

"Back, boys! Don't kill that man!"

Among them he plunged till he reached the side of Morrison, then turned and faced the brothers of his country and his State. With a downward stroke he arrested a saber thrust, and then struck upward at a rifle's mouth as it spit its deadly flame.

"Don't kill him! Do you hear?" he cried, as he beat

at the bayonet points. "I'm Cary! Herbert Cary!—
on the staff of General Lee!"

For an instant the attacking Southerners stood aghast
at the sight of this raging man in gray who defended a
Yankee officer; and yet he had made no saber stroke to
wound or kill; instead, his weapon had come between
their own and the life of a well-nigh helpless foe. For a
moment more they paused and looked with wondering
eyes, and in that moment their victory was changed to
rout.

A bugle blared. A thundering rush of hoof beats
sounded on the road, and the Union reënforcements
swept around the curve. Six abreast they came, a regiment of strong, straight riders, hungry for battle, hot to
retrieve the losing fortune of the day. The road was too
narrow for a concentrated rush, so they streamed into
the fields on either side, re-formed, and swept like an
avalanche of blue upon their prey. The guns in the
woods now thundered forth afresh, their echoes rolling
out across the hills, and the attacking Rebels turned and
fled, like leaves before a storm.

On one side of the road, Morrison and Cary shrank
down beside the wall to let the Union riders pass; on
the other, all that was left of the Rebel force ran helter-
skelter for a screen of protecting trees. But before the
last one disappeared he threw up his gun and fired, hap-
hazard, in the direction whence he had come.

As if in reply came the sound of a saber falling from

a man's hand and striking on a stone. Under his very eyes and just as he was putting out his hand to grip the others Morrison saw Herbert Cary sinking slowly to the ground.

And then, through the yellow dust clouds and the powder smoke and all the horrid reek of war, a child came running with outstretched arms and piteous voice —a frightened child, weeping for the father who had thrown himself headlong into peril to save another's life and who, perhaps, had lost his own.

Chapter Nine

The headquarters of the Army of the Potomac on the morning of August 4, 1864, were at City Point near where the Appomattox meets the James. Here the grim, silent man in whose hands lay the destinies of the United States sent out the telegrams which kept the Federal forces gnawing at the cage in which Lee had shut himself and meanwhile held to his strategic position south of Richmond. To his left and west lay Petersburg still unconquered, but Petersburg could wait, for Early's gray clad troopers were scourging the Shenandoah and the menace must be removed. To this end Grant had sent a telegram to Washington three days before expressing in unmistakable terms what he wished General Sheridan and his cavalry to accomplish. They were to go over into the Shenandoah and, putting themselves *south* of the enemy, follow him to the death. To which telegram the tall, lank, furrow-faced man in the White

House, whose kindly heart was bursting with the strain, replied in characteristic fashion and told him that his purpose was exactly right. And then, with a gleam of humor, warned him against influences in Washington which would prevent its carrying out unless he forced it.

This message had come but a few minutes before and it had been received with silent satisfaction for Grant knew now that Abraham Lincoln and he were in perfect accord as to the means for swiftly bringing on the end. But the plans must be well laid and to that end he must leave City Point within a few hours and go north. And so he was standing at a window of his headquarters this morning with his eyes resting unseeingly on the camp, while his cool, quiet mind steadily forged out his schemes.

Unlike the headquarters of "play" armies where all is noise and confusion and bloodied orderlies throw themselves off of plunging horses and gasp out their reports, the room in which General Grant did his work was strangely quiet.

It was a large, square room with high ceiling and wallpaper which had defied all the arts of Europe to render interesting in design. Furniture was neither plentiful nor comfortable—a slippery, black horse-hair sofa, a few horse-hair chairs and, at one side of the room, a table and a desk, littered with papers, maps and files. At the table Grant's adjutant, Forbes, sat writing. Fac-

ing him was the door opening out into the hallway of the house where two sentries stood on guard. In the silence which pervaded the room and in the quiet application to the work in hand there was a perfect reflection of the mind of him who stood impassive at the window with his back turned, a faint blue cloud of cigar smoke rising above his head.

A quick step sounded in the corridor—the step of one who bears a message. An orderly appeared in the doorway, spoke to the two sentries and was passed in with a salute to Forbes.

"For General Grant," he said, holding out a folded note of white paper. "Personal from Lieutenant Harris, sir."

At the sound of his name the General turned slowly and accepted the note which the orderly presented. He took it without haste and yet without any perceptible loss of time or motion and, as always, without unnecessary words. Scanning it, he shifted his cigar to one corner of his mouth where its smoke would not rise into his eyes, thought for an instant, then nodded shortly.

"I'll see him. At once."

Dismissed, the orderly saluted and passed quickly out. The General, with his chin in his collar and his cigar held between his fingers at nearly the same level, moved back to the window and stood there silently as before. He knew what Lieutenant Harris would wish to speak to him about. A few weeks before a Lieutenant-Colonel of cavalry had been court-martialed on the charge of allowing the escape of a spy. The court had found him guilty and its findings had been submitted to the higher authorities and endorsed by them. A copy of these reports now lay on his desk. All this his Adjutant, Forbes, knew as well as the General himself, but if Forbes had thought it worth while to speculate on the extent of his commander's interest he might have guessed for years without ever drawing one logical conclusion from all the hints that that impassive face and figure gave him.

Again a ringing step in the corridor and this time Lieutenant Harris came into the room, his hand going up in salute. But his General was still looking out of the window, his eyes on a dead level. There was a silence and then—without turning around—

"Well, Lieutenant, what is it?"

"A short conference, General, if you'll grant it. The case of Lieutenant-Colonel Morrison." It was hard work to talk to one who kept his back turned and Harris was embarrassed.

The smoke from the General's cigar still curled lazily upwards.

"Reprieve?" came the question.

Harris caught himself together and put all his feelings into his reply.

"No, General. A *pardon!*"

At once Grant wheeled and stood gazing at him keenly.

"*Pardon?*" he said, and he advanced with deliberation to the desk where he stood with his eyes steady on Harris' face. "Lieutenant! Do you want me to think you are out of your mind?"

Before Harris could reply Grant stopped him with a gesture and picked up a batch of papers which lay on the desk.

"The man has been given every chance. He has been court-martialed—and found guilty."

He dropped the papers in the case back on the desk. "And you—his counsel—having failed to prove him otherwise now come to *me*—for pardon."

He snapped his fingers. "Lieutenant, you are wasting time." And he turned away, pausing for a moment to turn over a sheaf here and there on his desk and meditate their contents. The incident of Lieutenant-Colonel Morrison has been disposed of and, in another moment would be forgotten. It was now or never for Harris and he answered quickly.

"I hope not, sir. Neither yours nor mine." And then, as the General looked up with some surprise at this retort, "You have read the findings of the court?"

"Yes," was the grim reply. "And approved the sentence. Tomorrow he will be shot."

"Yes, sir," acknowledged Harris. "Unless *you* intervene."

At this curiously insistent plea for clemency the short, stocky bearded man who, to so few, had the bearing of a great general, faced Lieutenant Harris and gave him a look which made the young officer's bravery falter for a long moment.

"*I?*" said the General, with a searching note in his voice which seemed to probe coldly and with deadly accuracy among the strenuous emotions in the young man's mind. "Harris—you are an officer of promise. Don't cut that promise short." With a flick of his ashes to one side he turned away. The cigar went back into the corner of his sardonic mouth.

Harris strode forward an impulsive step and threw out his hands.

"It is worth the risk. When a man is condemned to die—"

The General wheeled with more impatience than the Adjutant, Forbes, had seen him exhibit through many vexatious, worrying months. His voice took on a rasping note. He tapped the papers on the desk with grim significance.

"Lieutenant-Colonel Morrison has failed in his military duty. He released a Rebel spy—proved himself a traitor to his cause."

"A traitor, General?" protested the young officer. "Do you call a man a traitor who fought as Morrison did a week ago? Who stood his ground till his whole command was shot to pieces! And then stood alone—defending his colors in the face of hell let loose!"

The appeal was impassioned, its sincerity and humanity undoubted. Yet it seemingly only served to make the grim rules of war more unyielding than ever.

Choosing his words with more than ordinary care, and speaking them in firm, even tones, the General made his reply.

"No act of bravery can atone for a soldier's lapse from duty." He sat down at his desk and began to write.

Under ordinary circumstances Lieutenant Harris might have accepted defeat for there seemed no use in trying to break down that iron will or touch the heart of this relentless soldier. But this was something more than an ordinary case and Harris was more than simply Morrison's counsel—he was his friend. The two had fought together through three hard campaigns; they had shared food and water and shelter, had slept together for warmth on sodden fields, had exchanged such confidences as two officers from the same town in the North but of unequal rank may exchange under the pressure of wartime emotions. If there was one man living who knew Morrison's heart and appreciated his motives to the uttermost it was his lieutenant and the young officer was prepared to lose his commission, aye, even face prison for insubordination if continued opposition to the Commander-in-Chief would result in a re-hearing. And so he caught himself together for the second time and returned to the charge.

"I do not offer his courage as a plea for pardon," he said, and turned to his general with half a smile, "but still I find in Shakespeare—and in Blackstone—the suggestion of tempering justice with mercy."

Grant tossed aside his pencil, repeating the last word slowly, bitterly:

"*Mercy!*"

He rose from his seat and stood beside his table, speaking with a low but almost fierce intensity:

"They call me a war machine! I am! And you—and all the rest—are parts of it! A lever! A screw! A valve! A wheel! A machine half human—yes! A thing of muscle and bone and blood—but without a heart! A merciless *machine*, whose wheels must turn and turn till we grind out this rebellion to the dust of peace!"

He paused impressively, and in the hard, cold words which followed, all hope for Morrison seemed to fade and die.

"If a wheel once fails to do its work—discard it!—for another and a better one! *We want no wheels that slip their cogs!*"

The General ceased and turned to his littered table; but Harris was not yet beaten.

"No, General," he answered bravely, "but there happens to be a flaw . . . in your machine's control." The General looked up, frowning sharply; but Harris still went on: "In a military court we have condemned a man to die—*and the facts have not been proved!*"

Amazed more at the young officer's obstinate temerity than his words the General stared at him.

"How so?" he asked, with irony.

Harris opened out his hands with a simple gesture that seemed to leave his logic to the judgment of any impartial observer.

"In times of peace, my profession is that of the Law. I know my ground—and," in rising tones of sincerity, "I challenge you to shake it in any civil court in Christendom."

"Strong words, young man," came the stern reply. "For your sake, I hope they are warranted. What is your point? Get at it!"

Harris drew a short breath of relief. He had cleverly switched the appeal from grounds on which he stood no chance whatever to those where he did not fear any intellect in a fair fight.

"The evidence," he said calmly, "was purely circumstantial. In the first place, it is alleged that my client captured a Rebel spy, one Herbert Cary, who was hiding in the loft of a cabin."

The General's caustic tones interrupted. "To which fact," he said, "there were only *ten* witnesses."

"Yes, General," was the faintly smiling agreement. "Ten! But not one of them actually *saw* the man! They *believe* he was there, but they cannot swear to it."

Grant made a motion as of putting away something of no consequence. "Immaterial—in view of the other facts. Well—what else?"

"Next, it is claimed that Morrison released this spy

and allowed him to enter the Union lines—without regard to consequences."

The General gave a short exclamation of impatience,
and struck the papers on his desk with the flat of his
hand.

"And that is *proved*," he said, sharply. "Proved by
several officers who stopped your spy at points along the
road."

He singled out a soiled piece of paper from the sheaf
before him and held it up, a piece of paper which bore
writing on both sides.

"When taken, *this pass* was found on his person. Not
circumstantial evidence, but *fact*. Signed on one side
by R. E. Lee and, on the other, by Colonel Morrison."
He laughed shortly over the futility of argument under
such circumstances. "Do you presume to contest this,
too?"

To his amazement the young officer facing him bowed
easily and smiled in turn.

"I *do*. Emphatically. *No pass* was given Herbert
Cary either by Colonel Morrison *or* General Lee."

"*What?*" cried the General angrily.

Harris only pointed.

"Read it, sir—if you please." He watched till Grant's
eyes started to scan the pass again, and then repeated
the words which he knew so well.

"Pass *Virginia Cary* and escort through Federal—
and Confederate lines."

" 'Virginia Cary,' General, is a non-combatant and a child. 'Escort' may mean a single person—or it may mean a whole troop of cavalry."

To his infinite relief and joy his Commanding General looked up at him thoughtfully, then slowly rose from his desk and took a turn about the room, followed by a faint blue trail of cigar smoke. He paused.

"And what does *Cary* say?" he asked.

Again Harris smiled the quiet smile of the lawyer who has been confronted with such questions before and knows well how to answer them.

"He, too, is on trial for his life. His evidence, naturally, was not admitted."

"Ah! Then what says *Morrison*?"

"Nothing, sir," was the young lieutenant's calm reply. "The burden of proof lies with the prosecution—not with the defendant."

"And this is your contention—your *legal* flaw in my machine?" the General asked sharply.

"It is."

"Very good, sir—very good. In that case we'll call in these silent partners and dig into this case until we reach rock bottom!"

"Forbes," he ordered. "Send for the prisoner, Mr. Morrison—and the Rebel, Herbert Cary. I want both of them here—at once!"

In the pause which followed the Adjutant's exit Harris interposed an objection.

"Your method, General, is hardly just to the interests of my client."

Grant turned on him with something more than impatience. He was growing angry.

"Lieutenant Harris! Are you asking me to pardon a guilty man? It's the truth I want—not legal technicalities. Next you'll be asking me not to hang this Rebel spy because he has—a baby!"

He went back to his accustomed place at the window and stood looking out again, his hands clasped loosely behind his back, the eternal cigar smoke rising above his head. Then, to the young lieutenant's amazement, he asked a question in tones of ordinary conversation.

"Harris," he said. "Who was the man who preferred these charges to start with?"

"Corporal Dudley," was the eager answer.

"And there, General, is another point and a vital one that was not brought out. In reporting his Colonel, Dudley was actuated not by a spirit of military duty, but personal revenge."

"Revenge? Why?"

"Because Morrison shot and killed Dudley's brother —a Sergeant in his command."

The General came back from his window.

"Again—why?"

"For insubordination—incendiarism—attempted desertion," came the swift reply.

The General's eyebrows raised a fraction of an inch.

He seated himself at his desk and unrolled a map.

"Any witnesses of the Sergeant's death?" he asked evenly as he proceeded to study his map.

"Unfortunately, only one," Harris replied. "An old Negro—now in our camp—answering to the name of William Lewis."

"Lewis—Lewis," said Grant thoughtfully. He referred for a moment to a file of papers and then looked up. "Is that the old codger who's been worrying my entire staff for permission to go through our lines to his home?"

"Yes, General," said Harris, with a smile, for Unc' Billy's persistency and his troubles were known to everyone he met.

"Good! It's about time we got even him," the General remarked sardonically. "Have him in! See to it, Forbes." And again he bent over his map.

Forbes, passing out again, paused as Harris gestured.

"You'll find him somewhere near the guard house," the Lieutenant said with a flicker of a smile. "The old man has been regularly camping out there since he learned that his master was inside."

A minute passed and then, from a short distance away, came the sound of a squad of soldiers marching. In single file, with the two prisoners in line, the squad came into the hallway and stopped at the doorway.

"*Halt! Left face! Order arms! Prisoners file out!*"

The two prisoners stepped forward and entered the room.

Thanks to expert surgical work since he entered Union lines, Herbert Cary's wounds had healed quickly while plenty of good food had done the rest. His eyes may not have been bright with hope but at least they were clear with health and his straight back and squared shoulders showed that the man's fighting spirit had not left him even under the adverse decision of a court-martial.

Of the two, Morrison seemed the graver and quieter. With his sword taken from him and his shoulder straps ripped off the man who had been a Lieutenant-Colonel in the Army of the Potomac only the day before stood looking at his general without the slightest hope for clemency. Yet, with all the sad, quiet look of resignation in his eyes, behind them glowed a wonderful light— the light of self-sacrifice. For he had chosen to put on the tender glove of humanity and grip hands with the mailed gauntlet of war, and though he had been crushed yet even in this bitter hour they could not take from him the knowledge that the Commander-in-Chief of all spiritual armies would stand forever on his side. They could take his sword and shoulder straps but they could not rob him of that divine consolation.

And so the two stood with their eyes steady on the General—the Confederate, hard and defiant—the Union officer with a strange, sad glow on his face.

But the General paid them no attention. He was still studying the map laid out before him on his desk, the cigar in the corner of his mouth drawing one side of his face into harsh, deep lines. As a matter of fact, Ulysses Simpson Grant was very far removed from harshness—he was simply and solely efficiency personified. When nothing was to be said General Grant said nothing. To do otherwise was waste.

Presently he looked up and saw that while Forbes had given the two prisoners chairs directly in front of his desk one of the important factors in the business in hand had not been produced.

"Well, Forbes, well? Where is the Negro?" he asked crisply. "Bring him in! Bring him in!"

"In a moment, General," responded the Adjutant, hastening to the doorway as the tread of feet sounded again in the hallway. Dismissing the two privates who had arrived with Uncle Billy between them he led the old man down to the desk and left him there, bowing and scraping a little and holding his hat in front of him in both hands.

"Wan' see *me*, seh?" ventured Uncle Billy, intruding delicately on the General's calculations. "Here I is!"

General Grant looked up quickly and ran his eye over the old man.

"Your name!"

"Er—William Lewis, seh. Yas, seh."

"To whom do you belong?"

Although Uncle Billy's back was not particularly straight this sudden question introduced a stiffening into it which made it more upright than it had been in years.

"I b'longs to Cap'n Hubbert Cary, seh—of de Confed'it Army. Das who I b'longs to. Yas, seh."

The General sat back a little in his chair and studied Uncle Billy. He saw that after all the old Negro was simply a natural slave—that he probably had no other thought in his grayed head than that of faithful service to his owner. But he would try him and see how far the old man would go.

"I understand," he said, "that freedom has been offered you—and you refused it. Is this true?"

"Yas, seh."

"*Why?*" asked the General quietly.

Uncle Billy stammered.

"Well—er—well, 'skuse me, Mars' Gen'l, but—but down whar *I* lives at de—de white gent'men understands a nigger better'n what you-all does. Yas, seh."

General Grant may have smiled internally, but the only symptom of amusement was the dry note in his voice.

"I see. But there has been some difference of opinion on the point."

He paused and then pointed past Uncle Billy directly at Morrison. "Do you know that man?"

"Me?" said Uncle Billy. He turned and saw Morrison and instantly his face lighted up. It made no difference to the old Negro that Morrison's uniform was mutilated —he could only see the familiar features of one who had treated his dead mistress with perfect respect under trying circumstances.

"Aw, yas, seh," he broke out, with a broad grin. "How you does, Cun'l. I clar to—"

Uncle Billy stopped. His eyes had gone beyond Morrison to the man sitting beside him and at the sight of that loved figure the old man began to tremble. His voice lowered to a whisper and he began to totter forward.

"Mars' Cary!" he said, as if he were looking on one risen from the dead. He came a little nearer, with his hand stretched out as if to touch him testingly—then suddenly dropped down on his knees before Cary who had risen from his chair. "Bless Gawd, I done fin' you," he sobbed, his face buried in his master's coat. "I done fin' you at last."

The General frowned.

"Forbes," he ordered. "Put a stop to that. Bring him back!"

But Uncle Billy paid not a bit of attention as the Adjutant sprang up. All his thought was for his master and his own explanation.

"Dey wouldn' lemme git thru, seh!" he cried, pleading absolution from what had seemed an inexcusable breach of trust. "Dey wouldn' gimme no pass an' I'se

des been stuck! Aw, Gawd, Mars' Cary—an' I axed
'em ev'y day!"

"There now, Billy—don't," Cary said with a gesture
of pity and unending gratitude.

Uncle Billy rose slowly to his feet.

"Yas, seh. Yas, seh," he answered obediently. "'Skuse
me, Mars' Gen'l. I couldn' he'p it, seh. I—I couldn' he'p
it. Dey wouldn' eben lemme see him in de guard
house—"

"That will do," interrupted the General firmly. "Listen to me. When did you see Mr. Morrison—last?"

"Him?" said Uncle Billy, looking around at the Union
officer. "'Twas—'twas in de spring, seh. Yas, seh. De
time de Yankees bu'nt us out."

"How's that?" asked the General, not understanding.

Lieutenant Harris came forward a step.

"The act of incendiarism I spoke of, General—on the
part of Sergeant Dudley."

The General looked up and nodded.

"I see," he said, and Harris, knowing that due weight
would be given the fact let go a faint sigh of relief and
stepped back.

The cigar came out of the General's mouth. "Tell me
about it," he said to Uncle Billy.

The old Negro drew himself up and shifted his weight
onto his other foot.

"Well, seh, 'twas dis way. One mornin' de bluebellies—'skuse me, seh, de cav'lry gent'men. One mornin' de cav'lry gent'men come ridin' up, lookin' fer horses an' fodder an'—an' Mars' Cary—an' anything else what was layin' roun'. Yas, seh. An' des' befo' dis here gent'man come," with a bow at Morrison, "a low-lived white man took'n grab me by de th'oat—an' choke me, seh. Den he 'sult Miss Hallie—"

"Miss Hallie?" queried the General.

"My mis'tiss, seh," answered Uncle Billy. "My mis'tiss, seh," he said again and his hand went up to his eyes.

"The wife of Captain Cary," Harris said in a low tone and the General nodded.

"Den—bless Gawd—de Cun'l come! He pick him down off'n de front po'ch—and put him under 'rest. Yas, seh. An' Miss Hallie, she so' was hoppin', Gen'l. She—"

"Never mind that," sighed the man whose creed was Patience. "Go on with the story."

"Yas, seh. Thank'e, seh. 'Twas des lek I tell you, seh. An' arfter while orders come to de cav'lry gent'men fer to light out fr'm dar in a hurry. An' whilst dey was gettin' ready, seh, an' me an' de Cun'l was waitin' roun' fer to proteck de property, de fire bus' right out de winders!

"Dat's right, Mars' Gen'l," Uncle Billy hurried to state, as the General's eyebrows went up in surprise. "Dat's right. Den de front do' flewed open, an' here come dat po' white trash rapscallion—wid de pine knot in his han'. Yas, *seh*. He—"

"One moment!" snapped the General. "Was he running *towards* his troop or *away* from it?"

"*Way* fr'm it, seh," replied the old Negro, with unmistakable truthfulness, "t'odes de ice house whar Miss Hallie an' de chillun was at. Yas, seh."

"And Mr. Morrison tried to stop him?"

"Ha!" cried Uncle Billy, with a chuckle. "He mo'n tried, seh. He *done* it!"

The General nodded, his lips tight shut.

"So I understand. But what did he do—or say?"

At this question Uncle Billy suddenly developed dramatic abilities that his master had never dreamed of.

"He say—" and Uncle Billy's arm shot out as he pointed something deadly at an invisible foe—"he say, '*Halt! Dudley! Halt! Bang!*'"

Uncle Billy's hat dropped down on the floor with a whack. "Dat's all, seh. Dat po' white trash—he drop lek a stuck pig, seh!"

The General's eyes were on his desk and for a moment there was a pause. Finally, he lifted his head and looked at Morrison, who rose in salute.

"Mr. Morrison. You did well. Your Sergeant failed in his military duty—and deserved the punishment. I commend your action."

Harris, listening with all his might, thought the word more favorable than the tone in which they were spoken and his face brightened. Then he heard the General speaking more sternly.

"The Federal powers of administrative justice now occupy precisely the same position with regard to your own default."

Harris' face darkened. After the first just encomium —what was this that was coming?

Relentless and inflexible the voice went on.

"The rules of war, as applied to a non-commissioned officer, must also govern his superiors. As Sergeant Dudley deserved his bullet you merit *yours*."

His eyes dropped from Morrison's face and he looked up at Harris.

"A bad witness for your client, Lieutenant," he said grimly, as he nodded his head towards Uncle Billy. "You ought to study law! Take him away," and he picked up a fresh cigar from a box in front of him and tossed the old one out of the window.

Uncle Billy, with a puzzled look on his face, slowly yielded to the touch of the two soldiers who stepped into the room at a gesture from Forbes. He seemed to realize that his testimony had not been of much avail though just why was indeed a mystery. One thing, however, was quite clear.

" 'Skuse me, Mars' Gen'l. I—I don't need dat ar pass home now. An' I much obliged to you fer *not* givin' it to me. Yas, seh. Thank'e, seh." At the doorway he bowed with careful politeness to each occupant of the fatal room. "Good mornin', Mars' Cary. Good mornin', gent'- men. *Good* mornin'."

With the disappearance of bewildered Uncle Billy the General swung around on the officer who no longer wore his shoulder straps.

"Mr. Morrison," he said, in his distinct, even tones. "Your friend and counsel, Lieutenant Harris, has applied to me for your pardon!"

"*Pardon?*" cried Morrison, springing to his feet with an exclamation of amazement.

"Exactly," was the crisp response. "It comes from him—not from you. But still, as an interested party, have you anything to say in your own behalf?"

The Union officer stared at his general for a moment without replying. Yes, there were many things that might be said—all of them honest arguments in his own behalf, all of them weighted with Right and Humanity but none of them worth putting into words in the face of this deadly machine of war, this grim, austere, unyielding tribunal. He wavered for a moment on his feet as a terrible wave of despair surged over him, then made a faint gesture of negation.

"I have nothing to say, sir."

"Captain Cary!" ordered the General and, as Cary rose unsteadily to his feet, "No. Keep your seat, sir; you are wounded. Is it true—as I learn from this report— that during a skirmish a week ago you helped defend the Union colors against your own people?"

Cary shot up from his chair with a fiery rush of anger.

"*I? No, sir!* I defended the *man*—not the soldier, or his flag!"

"Ah!" ejaculated the General, leaning back in his chair and blowing out a cloud of smoke in surprise. "You draw a rather fine distinction, Captain. You saved the colors—*but you failed to save the man!* You had better have let him die—as an honorable soldier." There was silence for a moment, and the General asked: "Is it true that you were actuated by a debt of gratitude?"

"Yes," answered the Southerner, throwing back his head. "And a greater debt than I can ever hope to pay. His mercy to—my little girl."

Without relaxing for a moment his grip on the points of the case, no matter what human elements might be drawn into it, the General instantly rose and shot out an accusing forefinger at the Confederate.

"And the pass he gave—*to you!*"

Their eyes clashed but the Southerner lowered his own not a whit and backed them, furthermore, with honest anger.

"*To her!*" he answered, and drove the reply home with clenched jaws.

The General relaxed—and smiled.

"Another fine distinction," he said, resuming his seat. He knocked the ashes from his cigar and presently looked up with another one of those terribly vital questions which came so simply from his lips. "Did you ever penetrate the Federal lines by means of a uniform—of blue?"

The Confederate drew back as he felt the assault on his rights as a soldier.

"As to that, General Grant, there is—"

"Answer me!" came the sharp command. " 'Yes' or 'No'!"

"One moment, General," interrupted Harris, with a lawyer's quick objection. "If—"

"No interference, Harris," came the curt order. "Answer me, Captain. 'Yes' or 'No'!"

The Southerner's face flushed and he threw back his head with the superb defiance that General Grant knew so well—which was his one eternal stumbling block, and due to continue for another full year of blood.

"Under the rulings of court-martial law," the Confederate Captain said in ringing tones, "I deny even *your* right to the question."

To the surprise of everyone the General merely nodded.

"That is all, sir. Thank you," he said, and Cary, with a look of surprise, slowly resumed his seat.

"Mr. Morrison!"

The Union officer rose and saluted.

"As a military servant of the United States Government you were ordered to pursue this man and take him —dead or alive. In this you failed."

Morrison inclined his head gravely but shot a look of respectful objection at his superior.

"In part—I failed."

Instantly the accusing forefinger was leveled at him across the desk and the point made with terrible directness.

"*And knowing he was a spy!*"

Morrison shook his head.

"Not to my personal knowledge, sir. I hunted him many times; but never while he wore a Federal uniform."

"And when you captured him?"

In reply, Morrison simply indicated Cary's tattered coat of gray.

"Ah! Then you *did* capture him?"

"Yes," came the quiet answer.

"And he *was* the escort mentioned in your pass."

"Yes," Morrison answered slowly.

"H'm," said the General. He rose and turned to Harris.

"I am afraid, my dear Harris, that in spite of fine spun distinctions and your legal technicalities, the findings of our court were not far wrong."

Dropping his handful of papers on the desk he caught Morrison's eye and rasped out his analysis of the case.

"Captain Cary practically admits his guilt! *You* were aware of it! And yet you send him through the very center of our lines! A *pass!* Carte blanche to learn the disposition of our forces—our weakness and our strength—and to make his report in Richmond. He was an enemy—with a price on his head! And you trusted him! *A spy!*"

As the General had been speaking the first few words of his contemptuous summing up Morrison saw where they would lead and his manhood instantly leaped up in reply.

"I trusted, not the spy, but *Herbert Cary,*" he said with honest courage. Then, as the General turned his back on him with a contemptuous snap of his fingers—

"General! I have offered no defense. If the justice of court-martial law prescribes a firing squad—I find no fault. I failed. I pay."

With a gesture which indicated Cary the disgraced officer of the Army of the Potomac shot out his one and only defense of his action—at an unyielding back.

"I took this man—hunted—wounded—fighting to reach the side of a hungry child. I captured him and, by the rules of war, I was about to have him shot. Then he asked me to get his little girl safely to Richmond, and not to let her know—about him."

"And she believed in *me. Trusted* me—even as I trusted Herbert Cary to pierce the very center of your lines—as a father—not a spy!"

From behind the unyelding back came a statement of fact, firm and pitiless.

"And it cost you your sword—your life."

Morrison centered his eyes on the back of the General's head and sent his answer home with all the power of his voice and spirit.

"And I have no regret," he said. "In the duty of a military servant—I have failed. But my prisoner still lives! I could *not* accept the confidence of his child—the trust of innocence—a baby's kiss—with the blood of her father on my hands!" He dropped his hands and half turned away.

The General turned, a little at a time—first his head and then his shoulders.

"A very pretty sentiment," he remarked dryly. "But you seem to forget that we are not making love but *war.*"

With a supreme burst of anger at his helplessness before the brute forces which would presently send him forth to the firing squad, Morrison wheeled on his commanding general and flared forth with his last reply.

"Yes, *war!* And the hellish laws that govern it. But there is another law—*Humanity!* Through a trooper in my command the home of an enemy was turned to ashes—his loved ones flung out to starve. When a helpless tot had lost its mother and a father would protect it, then *war* demands that I smash a baby's one last hope—in the name of the Stars and Stripes. And then—to march back home, to a happy, triumphant North—and meet *my* baby—with the memory of a butcher in my heart—*By Heaven, sir! I'd rather hang!"*

For a moment General and Colonel regarded each

other fixedly and then the General turned away to pace the floor. Presently he came to his decision and walked slowly back to his desk.

"Lieutenant Harris," he said in tones whose significance could not be misunderstood, "I was right. You have wasted your time—and mine."

Then he sighed wearily and made a last gesture to Forbes.

"*The guard,*" he said.

It was all over.

And then, to the ears of the two prisoners who stood looking at one another with sad eyes, came a sound which made both men start and look again with apprehension written on their faces—the shrill scream of a child who is being kept from something she has set her heart upon. Another moment and there was a rush of tiny feet in the hall, whereupon the two sentries crossed their rifles across the doorway. But what might have proved a serious obstruction for a man was only an absurdity to a child's quick wit and Virgie, with a little duck of her sunny head, dodged quickly under the muskets and charged, flushed and panting, on the General's desk.

"You shan't shoot Colonel Morrison," cried this astonishing newcomer in tones of shrill command as she stamped her little foot: "I won't let you! You shan't! You shan't!"

A moment of displeased surprise on the part of the General. Then—

"Take the child out of here," he ordered.

"I won't *go!*" answered Virgie, tossing her curls back and standing her ground with angry eyes.

"Orderly!" called the General.

With a whirl Virgie dashed away from the desk, eluded the orderly and threw herself into her father's arms.

"Oh, Daddy, Daddy! You won't let him shoot the Colonel. Daddy, you won't! You won't!" She burst into a passionate flood of tears.

Cary lifted his hand to the General in a plea for a moment's respite from force.

"General—please. She'll go."

He turned to the sobbing child and shook her gently. "Virgie! Virgie! Listen, honey! *Remember General Lee!*" The bowed head rose from her father's shoulder; the little shoulders stiffened, and eye to eye she looked into the face of Cary as his pleading voice went on: "*He* wouldn't want you to cry like this. He said—'She's a brave little soldier to stay there all alone. Dixie and I are *proud* of her.'"

The Littlest Rebel's chin went up, and she bravely choked back her sobs. If this was what her General wanted, this her General would have, though childhood's sobs are hard to check when a little heart is aching for the pain of those she loves.

"Go now, darling," her father pleaded. "Go."

She kissed him, and turned in silent, slow obedience, casting a scowl at the grim and silent General Grant, then moved toward the guarded door.

"Wait!" said a quiet voice.

"Harris! They say that fools and children speak the truth." He paused and then said gently: "Come here, little girl. Come here and talk to me."

Somewhat in fear now that the kind voice robbed her of her anger the little pale faced child choked down her sobs and came slowly forward to the desk. But, as she stood there, her courage returned and, marvel of marvels, her tiny hand went up in imitation of a salute.

Grant dropped his chin in his hand so that their heads were nearly on a level across his desk and looked at her with gentle kindness in his eyes.

"The Littlest Rebel, eh?" he said in low tones. "How old are you?"

"S-s-seven. Goin' on eight," responded Virgie, gulping down a sob and nervously fingering her tattered dress.

"Ah, yes," he nodded. "And do you know the uniform of a Union officer—when you see it?"

Virgie's small mouth dropped open at the absurdity of the question and she almost laughed.

"A Yankee?" she queried with scorn. "Well, I reckon I *ought* to—by *this* time."

"Very good," the brown bearded man nodded, and

gently blew smoke at the ceiling. "Now, tell me. When you lived at home—and afterwards in your cabin—did your father come to see you often?"

Virgie's sunny head nodded in emphatic asseveration. "Yes, sir. Often."

"*How* often?" asked the bearded man.

Virgie's fingers twisted themselves deep in her dress. "I—I don't know, sir. But heaps of times."

"Good again," and the questioner actually smiled. "When your father came, did he ever wear clothes that —that were not his own?"

Virgie turned a sidelong look on her father but, as he could not help, her puzzled eyes went back to the General.

"Well—well, lots of our men don't have hardly *any* clo's," she said pathetically.

Another smile broke the sternness of the General's face.

"That isn't what I mean," he explained gently. "Did he ever wear a coat of blue—a *Yankee* uniform?"

"General!" broke in Harris.

"Lieutenant!" Grant frowned. He turned back to Virgie and coaxed her a little.

"Well? Tell me!"

With one bare big toe twisted under her foot and fingers interlocked in agony the child turned a look of pure anguish on her silent, grave faced father. This was torture—and she could not escape.

"Oh, Daddy, Daddy!" she burst forth with a wail of tragedy in her voice. *"What must I tell him?"*

The father's lips, which had been closed against the pain that racked him, softened with the perfect trust which went into his gentle command.

"The *truth*, Virgie. Whatever the General asks."

The General's observant eyes rested on the proud Southerner for an instant, noted that his face was quite without anxiety, then went back to the little child.

"Well, did he?" he asked.

"Y-y-yes, sir," answered Virgie with a gulp.

The General nodded and his face grew grave again.

"I wonder if you even know what it means. A *spy!*"

"Yes, sir," said the Littlest Rebel, and dropped her eyes.

"Hm. And do you remember how many times he came that way?"

"Yes, sir," came the instant answer, and she threw up her head. *"Once."*

"Once?" echoed the General, surprised. "Are you sure?"

"Yes, sir," she answered. She drew herself up proudly, forgetting the poor, tattered dress, and her clear eyes rested fearlessly on two others that read through them down into the pure whiteness of her soul.

"Think!" said the quiet voice again, while the perspiration started out on the forehead of more than one lis-

tener. "And remember what your father said just now. When was it?"

Again the fearless eyes of the child, the Littlest Rebel of them all, rose to the gaze of the man whose iron heel was crushing them into the ground and she made her answer—as crystal clear and truthful as if she stood before the Throne on the last great day.

"When—when Daddy came through the woods an'—an' put my mamma in the ground."

There was a silence. No one moved. Outside in the trees and bushes the song the summer insects were singing suddenly burst upon their ears and the myriad noises of the camp, hitherto unnoticed, became a veritable clamor, so complete was the stillness in the room. Everyone except perhaps the child herself realized the vital importance of her answer and now that it had been given the crisis had passed. The Littlest Rebel had put an end to questioning. An audible sigh went up from everyone except the man behind the desk.

This one turned his head slowly towards the Confederate prisoner.

"Captain Cary, is this true?"

"Yes, General," came the straightforward answer. "I went to your nearest post with a flag of truce and asked permission to go to my dead wife. I was refused. I went *without* permission."

General Grant rose to his feet. Centering the other's eyes with his own he spoke to him as one officer speaks to another when he expects the truth and nothing but the truth.

"And you give me your word, as a soldier and a gentleman, that once—once *only*—you wore a Federal uniform and that because of the burial of your wife?"

"I do," answered Herbert Cary, a rebel to the last. "And that was the only cause in heaven or hell that could have *induced* me to wear it!"

For a moment the Commander of the Army of the Potomac surveyed the still defiant prisoner, then turned his back and walked to the window where he tossed away a much chewed cigar, meantime thinking out his last analysis.

Here was a man who had been hunted tirelessly month after month as a rebel spy. It was true that he was a spy and true that he had worn a uniform of blue. Yet the fact had been established—by the spotless honesty of a little child—that he had worn the uniform only so that he might reach his home and bury his dead. And —went on the cool, quiet mind—since the man was *not* a spy how could a Union officer be executed for assisting a *spy* to escape?

Coming back to his desk again the General picked out another smoke, felt of it thoughtfully, sniffed at it, then raised his quiet eyes.

"Lieutenant-Colonel Morrison," he said in clear, incisive tones, "go back to your command!"

Five words. Five short, plain words, yet they made all

the difference between a firing squad and a chance at life again. There was a silence—then a gasp from Morrison's dry throat. At the sound of his title—at the sound of that blessed order which, by right of supreme power, instantly restored him to his rank, the Union officer leaped to his feet with a cry of joy. But it was not even for those around him in that little room to know the wonderful vista of happiness which opened up again before the eyes which only a moment ago had been doomed to close in the sleep of a disgraceful death.

The General's hand went up in a gesture which checked his gratitude.

"The *next* time you are forced to decide between military duty and humanity—think twice!"

He turned to his desk and took up a small piece of paper, crumpled and torn.

"Captain Cary," he said, "I sincerely regret that I cannot honor the pass as given you by Colonel Morrison," and he turned the paper over, "but I do honor the pass of your General—R. E. Lee."

He folded the paper and held it out to Cary who came forward as if in a dream. Then the General turned his back again and began to rummage on his desk. The incident was closed.

But there was a rush of bare, childish feet and before he could escape Virgie's brown little arms were round him and her dimpled chin was pressed against his waist.

The General made no effort to release himself but

looked down on her with a softer light in his face than any of his men had seen there in many months.

"And as for you, young lady, the next time you pervert my officers and upset the discipline of the Federal Army —well, I don't know *what* I'll do with you."

He looked down into her face and read there a wistful feminine appeal for outward and visible reconciliation.

"Oh, well," he said with mock resignation, "I suppose I've got to do it," and he stooped and kissed her. Then he took up his campaign hat and walked towards the door.

Behind him the child in her tattered dress and bare brown legs stood still and threw out her arms to him in a last soft-voiced good-by.

"Thank you, Gen'ral," called the Littlest Rebel, with the light of heaven in her eyes. "Thank you for Daddy and Colonel Morrison and *me*. You're another mighty good damn Yankee!"

And then, with a cry of surpassing joy and love, she rushed back to where the two men waited for her on their knees.

Chapter Ten

In the shade of a fringe of trees that edged the river bank a troop of cavalry was drawn up in one long, thin line. Knee to knee, the silent, blue-coated riders sat, waiting, waiting—not for a charge upon the enemy, or orders for a foray through an already harried land. They waited for a leader—a man who had led them through the heat and cold, through peaceful valleys and the bloody ruck of battle; a man whom they loved and trusted, fearing him only when they shirked a duty or disobeyed the iron laws of war.

This man had been taken from them, himself a servant who had disobeyed these laws, his sword dishonored, his shoulder straps ripped off before their eyes. And now the troopers waited—and for what? An order had come which put them on review, a long, thin line of horsemen waiting on the river bank, while the sun beat down on the parched red fields, and the waters of the muddy James lazed by as they murmured their sad, low song.

The troopers were silent—waiting. A horse stamped idly in the dust, and a saber rattled against a booted leg. A whisper ran down the line. The eyes of the men turned slowly at the sight of a single rider who advanced from the distant Union camp. He did not take the dusty road which swept in a wide, half-circle to where the waiting troopers sat in line, but jumped a low wormfence and came straight across the fields.

An officer he was, erect in his saddle, chin up and shoulders squared. On his shoulders his straps had been replaced, and his saber rattled against his thigh to the rise and fall of his horse's stride.

Straight on he came till he checked his mount before the center of the waiting line, and the troopers knew that Lieutenant-Colonel Morrison had once more come into his own.

Their sabers rasped from out the scabbards and rose in a joyous, swift salute, while Morrison's once dishonored sword acknowledged it.

" 'Tention . . . company!"

The long line stiffened and waited for their officer to speak; yet the voice was not the voice of an officer in command, but that of a comrade and a friend.

"Thank you, boys! It's good to be back again." He swallowed something in his throat and struggled manfully to speak in even tones. "I must ask you to be quiet —and not to—"

He stopped. Again his troop had disobeyed him—disobeyed him to a man. A shout went up, deep, joyous and uncontrolled, its echoes pulsing out across the hot, red fields till it reached the distant camp; and Grant looked up from a war map's crisscross lines, grunted, and lit a fresh cigar.

And Lieutenant-Colonel Morrison sat his horse before his cheering line of men, silent, happy, while two tears rolled, unheeded, down his cheek—a soldier and a man!

His tenderness to a little child had torn him from his saddle and doomed him to disgrace and death; and then, one line from her baby lips had mounted him again and set him before his troopers on parade.

"*It was when . . . Daddy came through the woods . . . and put my mamma . . . in the ground.*"

Two lives she had held—in her little hands—and had saved them both with a dozen words of simple, unfaltering truth.

.   .   .   .

On the dusty pike which led to Virginia's capital another rider plodded through the heat and haze. His coat, once gray, now hung in mud-stained tatters about his form, but beneath his battered campaign hat his thin, pale features were smoothed by a smile of happiness.

Behind his saddle, one hand gripped tightly in a rent in the soiled gray coat, sat still another Rebel—the smallest of them all—her tiny legs stretched out almost straight on the horse's wide, fat back.

"Daddy—how far is it to Richmon' now?"

The rider turned his head and pointed north.

"It's close now, honey. See that line of hills? That's Richmond. A mile or two and we'll be at home."

Again they plodded on, past fields of shriveled corn whose stalks stood silently in parched and wilted lines —lines that were like the ranks of the doomed Confederacy—its stalks erect, yet sapped of the juice of life. Where orchards once had flourished their rotted branches now hid mouths of rifle pits, and low, red clay entrenchments stretched across the fields.

"Daddy," broke out a piping voice, "don't you think we'd better make this Yankee horse get up a little? 'Cause—'cause somethin' *else* might happen before we get there."

"It's all right, Virgie," her father answered, with a pat on her small, brown knee. "These lines are ours, and I reckon we are safe at last."

They were. Two Rebels on a Yankee horse soon made their triumphant entry into Richmond. They passed through Rockets, by the half-deserted wharves on the river bank where a crippled gunboat lay, then clattered over the cobblestones up Main Street till they reached the Square. On the State House the Stars and Bars still floated; but the travelers did not pause. Northward they turned, then westward again, till they stopped at last before a silent, stately mansion, the headquarters of their General—General Lee.

Before the open door two sentries stood, but as Cary and his charge dismounted an orderly came down the steps and out of the iron gate. A word or two from Cary and the orderly disappeared into the house, returning soon with word that the visitors would be received—at once.

Up the stone steps went Virgie, holding tightly to her father's hand, for now, as she neared her General, her little heart was pounding, and her breath came eagerly and fast.

On the threshold of a dim and shaded room they paused and looked. He sat there, at a table strewn with war maps and reports—a tall gray man in a coat of gray —the soldier and the gentleman.

As father and child came in he rose to meet them, looking at the two with eyes that seemed to hold the sadness and the tenderness of all the world.

He knew their story; in fact, he had bent his every effort to the saving of Cary's life. He had sent a courier to the camp of General Grant below the city, asking a stay of sentence till the facts in the case were cleared; and only a half hour before his courier had returned with news of the prisoner's release.

And now, as he advanced and gave a courtly welcome to his trusted scout, the hand of the Littlest Rebel once more went up in salute to a superior officer.

"Gen'ral," she said, as she stole a glance at her father's smiling face, "I've brought him back—with—with the pass you gave me, sir."

And the General stooped—six feet of him—till his lips were on a level with Virgie's lips; then folded her closely into his great gray arms.

PEACE

Hushed is the rolling drum. The bugle's note
   Breathes but an echo of its martial blast;
The proud old flags, in mourning silence, float
   Above the heroes of a buried past.
Frail ivy vines 'round rusting cannon creep;
   The tattered pennants droop against the wall;
The war-worn warriors are sunk in sleep,
   Beyond a summons of the trumpet's call.

Do ye still dream, ye voiceless, slumbering ones,
   Of glories gained through struggles fierce and long,
Lulled by the muffled boom of ghostly guns
   That weave the music of a battle-song?
In fitful flight do misty visions reel,
   While restless chargers toss their bridle-reins?
When down the lines gleam points of polished steel,
   And phantom columns flood the sun-lit plains?

A breathless hush! A shout that mounts on high
   Till every hoary hill from sleep awakes!

Swift as the unleashed lightning cleaves the sky,
   The tumbling, tempest-rush of battle breaks!
The smoke-wreathed cannon launch their hell-winged shells!
   The rattling crash of musketry's sharp sound
Sinks in the deafening din of hoarse, wild yells
   And squadrons charging o'er the trampled ground!

Down, down they rush! The cursing riders reel
   'Neath tearing shot and savage bayonet-thrust;
A plunging charger stamps with iron heel
   His dying master in the battle's dust.
The shrill-tongued notes of victory awake!
   The black guns thunder back the shout amain!
In crimson-crested waves the columns break,
   Like shattered foam, across the shell-swept plain.

A still form lies upon the death-crowned hill,
   With sightless eyes, gray lips that may not speak.
His dead hand holds his shot-torn banner still—
   Its proud folds pressed against his bloodstained cheek.

O slumbering heroes, cease to dream of war!
   Let hatreds die behind the tread of years.
Forget the past, like some long-vanished scar
   Whose smart is healed in drops of falling tears.
Keep, keep your glory; but forget the strife!
   Roll up your battle-flags so stained and torn!
Teach, teach our hearts, that still dream on in life,
   To let the dead past sleep with those we mourn!

From pitying Heaven a pitying angel came.
   Smiling, she bade the tongues of conflict cease.
Her wide wings fanned away the smoke and flame,

Hushed the red battle's road. God called her Peace.
From land and sea she swept mad passion's glow;
   Yet left a laurel for the hero's fame.
She whispered hope to hearts in grief bowed low,
   And taught our lips, in love, to shape her name.

She sheathed the dripping sword; her soft hands pres't
   Grim foes apart, who scowled in anger deep.
She laid two grand old standards down to rest,
   And on her breast rocked weary War to sleep.
Peace spreads her pinions wide from South to North;
   Dead enmity within the grave is laid.
The church towers ring their holy anthems forth,
   To hush the thunders of the cannonade.

EDWARD PEPLE.